RETRIBUTION HIGH

Explicit Version

A Short, Violent Novel about Bullying, Revenge, and the Hell known as High School

by

Bob Gale

Retribution High – Explicit Version

A Short, Violent Novel about Bullying, Revenge,
and the Hell Known as High School

First Edition – October 2013

ISBN 978-0-9910415-3-4

Published by Big Wind Productions

The characters and events in this book are fictitious.
Any similarity to real persons, living or dead, is coincidental
and not intended by the author.

Cover by Samo Gale

A Note About This Version

Note: *Retribution High* is available in two versions, **Explicit** and **Standard**. This is the **Explicit Version.** It contains dialogue laced with profanity, sexual references, hot-word epithets, and hurtful gay bashing. As a movie, it would definitely be rated "R." If you're offended by profanity, you should be reading the Standard Version, which contains none of the 68 words or expressions forbidden on network television.

For anyone who has ever been
harassed or hurt by a bully.

You are not alone.

Sometimes God answers prayers

and sometimes the devil does.

- Italian Proverb

Chapter 1

There was one word that best described the 45-year old man in the $1500 suit, the $150 tie, the $600 shoes and the $235 haircut who arrogantly entered the office of the Principal of Woodrow Wilson Public High School on that Monday October morning. The word was *asshole*.

Frank Niles had been called many other things throughout his life, both to his face and behind his back. He had been called these things by his associates, by his employees, by his clients, by his enemies, by his family and by his ex-wife (especially by his ex-wife), things like bully, sleazeball, scumbag, shyster, dickhead and motherfucker. But *asshole* most succinctly summed him up. Yet Frank Niles didn't care. He didn't care because he *was* an asshole -- a bully whose power and wealth enabled him to kick almost anyone else's ass. So if people didn't call him those things, he'd be concerned that he wasn't kicking hard enough.

It should be no surprise, then, to learn that Frank Niles was a lawyer, a lawyer whose clients were often called the same things that he was.

Principal Louise Jones, PhD, was well aware of who Frank

Niles was. She knew immediately that he hated her as soon as he stepped into her office. He hated her because she was not just a woman in power, but a black woman in power. He hated her because she had power over his son. And most of all, he hated her because she wielded just enough power to make him come to her.

And Frank Niles immediately knew she hated him. Public servants always hated him – if they didn't, he wouldn't be Frank Niles. He'd seen her type before, in the schools from which his son had been expelled. She was the career educator who had gotten her teaching credentials, oh, some three decades ago, with the intent to make the world a better place. And she *had* tried to do just that, only to get beaten down by a system that thwarted her at almost every turn. Her spartan office, with the worn furniture, the cracks in the wall, and the frayed carpeting told him she practiced what she preached. The tax dollars that went to "Woody" High weren't spent on the administrators. Admirable. She was a public servant who couldn't be bought. Even with all of her lost battles, she still cared about her students. He could see those lost battles in the lines in her face and in the sag of her shoulders. But she was not a woman who won very often. Then again, for her, surviving was victory enough. Surviving meant she got to keep her job, which meant she would get her pension in another few years and she'd never have to deal with parents like Frank Niles again. Which meant that Frank Niles had the advantage, even on her turf.

He glared at her. "So why am I here, Mizzzzzz Jones?

Obviously it's about my son, but what, exactly?"

"It's *Doctor* Jones, Mr. Niles. Please be seated."

There was only one chair that he could sit in, she'd made sure of that, just one chair without books and papers stacked on it. It was the overstuffed chair she used for meetings with parents like Frank Niles, as well as for meetings with students who had parents like Frank Niles. You sat down in that chair and you sank down a little too far, just far enough that you'd have to look up at Doctor Louise Jones from across her desk. Frank Niles had a similar chair in his office. The intimidation chair.

He sat down, sank down, but his face betrayed no surprise. He was not one to be intimidated, certainly not by a school bureaucrat or her chair.

Doctor Jones swiveled her computer screen around so that he could see it. "Take a look at these web pages."

The screen showed a blog page called ***Hard Woody 411*** which Frank Niles had never seen before. The graphics were slick, and it was laid out like a tabloid, with a screaming headline, a photo with cycling animation, and an "article."

This one had a photo of an ordinary looking girl accompanied a headline, **IS EMILY "SLUT" GARDINO THE NEW BLOW JOB QUEEN?** After a beat, her mouth formed a big fat "O" and bobbed back and forth. Humiliating. Frank Niles was glad this wasn't his daughter.

Doctor Jones clicked her mouse.

The next edition headline read, **MITCH "WHEEZER" SIMON – ASTHMA OR JUST FULL OF MUCUS?** A photo of a nerdy boy was accompanied by some snorting sound effects as animated green phlegm poured from his nostrils in a torrent. Disgusting.

Click!

KAREN LANE WEARS VIBRATOR PANTIES! A head shot of Karen was grafted onto an animated cartoon body that precisely illustrated the headline. Embarrassing.

Click!

"LARD ASS" FOLEY'S PIZZA FACE SETS NEW RECORD FOR ZITS! The fat kid's acne face broke out in multiplying pimples which then erupted in pus. Gross.

Click!

POLL: CLAIRE HEDRICK IS THE UGLIEST SKANK AT WOODY! The photo of an extremely unattractive girl was grafted onto the body of Godzilla in video footage showing screaming people running from the monster. Degrading.

Click!

SEPARATED AT BIRTH? CAN YOU TELL THESE SOWS APART? The accompanying photos showed an overweight girl next to an obese hog. Both of them made pig noises. Insulting.

Click!

WHEEZER AND SHRIMPBOAT: THE RUNTS MUST

BE FAGS! The image showed the mucus-faced nerd with another kid, animated in some suggestive and unflattering positions together.

It was lewd, and Frank Niles had seen more than enough. He swiveled the screen back around to the Principal. "Okay, it's a high school version of the National Enquirer. And I presume my son is the subject of one of these?"

"No, we believe your son is *responsible* for all of these."

Frank Niles snorted, but Doctor Jones couldn't tell if this was a laugh or a reaction of disgust.

"*This* is why you called me here?" he thundered. "For juvenile gossip? In my day, we spread it by phone, or on bathroom walls or in underground flyers. Same thing, different medium."

"Then you approve?" she asked, in disbelief.

"Certainly not. But kids are kids. They do dumb, immature, sometimes nasty things. If you're so bothered by it, just shut down the website."

"We can't. It's not set up through the school."

"Then it's private enterprise and freedom of expression. And freedom of expression is protected by the first amendment. You still teach the first amendment, don't you?"

"I think this goes beyond 'freedom of expression.' I think we're into hate speech and maliciousness."

"Whatever happened to "sticks and stones can break my bones but words can never hurt me?""

"But words *can* hurt, Mr. Niles. Kids can be branded with a label in high school that follows them the rest of their lives. It can lead to failure, depression, drug abuse. Last year, a girl here attempted suicide as result of this sort of harassment..."

She put a file folder in front of him with the name "Dana Madison." But Frank Niles ignored it and stood up, very intense.

"Ma'am, if you're making an accusation against my son, you'd better show me some hard evidence. Otherwise, you're simply engaging in the same sort of sleazy gossip and innuendo you're accusing Doug of."

"Mr. Niles, I'm not a lawyer --"

"Well, *I am*. And you -- and your school board -- would be very wise to remember that."

"Please, Mr. Niles, there's no reason to make threats. I simply thought that you might have a conversation with Doug about this. Surely, you don't seen any value in it."

"Doug lives with his mother. Talk to her."

"I've tried, but she's canceled six appointments."

"That's because she's a flake and a selfish bitch -- which is why I divorced her."

Doctor Jones smirked. That was not the version that had been reported by the local news media. That version involved him, some under-aged call girls, a "Gentlemen's Club" and some cocaine, and it was why Doug had been rejected by every private school in the area.

"Mizzzz Jones, I don't get to see my son very often. When I do, the last thing I want to do is antagonize him with some rumors. So, in the future, don't call me unless my son has actually done something. And by that, I mean something *serious*."

And with that, Frank Niles left the building.

Louis Jones sighed. Like father, like son. It was game over, and she'd lost. She'd lost before she could even use all of her ammunition. 18 years ago there had been a lawsuit against the school district which had destroyed the possibility of any serious discipline. Political correctness cut both ways, and that lawsuit had cut the heart out of the school district's ability to enforce the most basic standards, both behavioral and academic. Now, unruly students needed to be "understood," not punished, even as they made learning impossible in the classes they disrupted. Now, no was ever expelled. Now, no one ever failed. In fact, now, no one ever got less than a C minus. Doctor Louise Jones had summoned Frank Niles in hopes that the threat of publicizing Doug's website and the embarrassment of tying him to it might make him do what she could not. But she'd been foolish to think that a man who had weathered so many scandals could ever be embarrassed. Her only other real option was to publicize the matter and involve the press, law enforcement and local politicians. But many of those politicians could be bought by men like Frank Niles, and such a move would put her into conflict with the School Board and their policy affectionately known as "don't make waves." And Louise

Jones had her pension to think about.

She slumped in her chair in defeat. She looked at the image of the two boys, “Shrimpboat” and “Wheezer” on the screen. Two innocent boys who had never done any harm to anyone. Two innocent boys who simply had the misfortune to be smaller than the rest of their classmates. Two innocent boys whom she had just condemned to another school year in hell, a year that might result in scars – physical, emotional and/or spiritual – which would never heal and which could possibly ruin their lives.

She closed her eyes and sighed. “May God protect you poor kids. Because the school certainly can't.”

She sincerely hoped God was listening.

Chapter 2

Woodrow Wilson Public High School was a clean, landscaped school in Westover, a far outer suburb of Kansas City, Kansas. It had been built in the '90s and, from outward appearances, it looked like a nice, safe place for a kid. Just like Columbine.

Westover had, what the government would term, a "diverse economic population." That meant there were rich people, poor people, and everyone in between. The town had originally been trailer parks and ramshackle working class houses, serving factories that had long since shuttered. In the 1980s, white flight from the big city and cheap land resulted in the construction of numerous middle-class and upper middle-class subdivisions, as well as the Westover Mall, a skating rink, and eventually Woody High. Given this history – or lack thereof – Westover was not a community brimming with civic pride. There wasn't much to be proud of, and Woody's mediocre sports teams didn't help. People lived there, but worked somewhere else. They led their own lives, minded their own business and, just like the school board they elected, didn't make waves.

When the 3:00 bell rang at Woody High, it meant freedom and relief for most of the kids. But not for those two boys Doctor

Jones was worried about. Not today.

Jordy "Shrimpboat" Hubbard and Mitch "Wheezer" Simon were both 16, both smaller than average, and both a bit behind in puberty. They had no facial hair, none on their chests, and their voices hadn't changed. They both shared a birthday: August 17. Jordy's nickname was a result of his short stature, and Mitch's was a result of his asthma. All their lives they'd been among the last picked on any sports team, and neither had a father figure in their lives. This combination of things had made them friends...and easy targets for the jocks and jerks. And when you're a target, you're shunned by everyone else, because if you associate with a target, you become a target too. So the boys didn't have many other friends. At least they weren't truly hated – after all, it's hard to hate the little guys, even when they're a bit unkempt and awkward. And they never did anything to make them worth hating. No, they were mocked and targeted for what they were, not for what they did. Because all they were ever doing was trying to survive in that hellish, sadistic pressure cooker of social insanity called "high school."

As Mitch made his way to his locker, he pulled out his inhaler, only to have it knocked out of his hand by someone running past him.

"What's wrong, Wheezer, can't breathe? Too bad! You're missing the smell of my farts!"

It was "Big-E" Edwards, a certified jerk who had once

jumped Mitch in a bathroom stall and given him a swirlie so bad that he had to be taken to the emergency room. Mitch let him disappear, then scrambled down the hall to where the inhaler landed, and checked before bending over to pick it up. Safe. Mitch took a snort, cleared his breathing passages and continued to his locker.

Jordy fared worse. “Vomit” Greene ambushed him from around the corner with a shaken can of Coke and sprayed Jordy's crotch, then sang with all the maturity of an 8-year old, “Shrimpboat pissed his pa-ants! Shrimpboat pissed his pa-ants!” It was hardly any consolation to Jordy that no one but Greene thought it was funny -- Jordy's pants were still wet, and Vomit would never pay for his crime.

The boys approached their lockers from opposite directions. They were eight lockers apart in another accident of fate that suggested that their lives were intertwined. Eight. They'd been eight years old when they first met, they were born in the eighth month, on the 17th, which was one and seven which equals eight. As they neared their lockers, their stomachs tightened and their expressions turned to dismay as they spotted the familiar long red cards sticking out of them with those three dreaded words: “You've Been Invited.” Shit. *Not again.*

They walked down the main steps of the school like condemned men. The weight of their backpacks was nothing compared to the weight of those cards. They knew the drill.

Carry the red cards so everyone could see them. Carry the red cards so everyone could see who today's target was. Some kids laughed and taunted them. "The fags got invites again!" "Sucks to be you!" "Can't wait to see you turds on the 411!" The kids on the bus, their bus, the bus they *would* have been on, were no less charitable. "At least the bus won't stink today!" "Hey, I'll save your seats – so my dog can shit on 'em!" Others looked away, preferring to ignore the entire concept and find bliss in their bogus ignorance. Like their parents, these kids chose not to be involved. It was safer that way, and in high school, it was all about self-preservation. Then there were those who had received invitations in the past – and might very well receive them in the future – who looked at them with expressions of empathy mixed with "at least it's not me today."

And then there was Amy Danforth. Amy was one of the few who looked at them with honest-to-God sympathy. She was one of the few who actually talked to them. Amy had gone through grade school with them, and then junior high school. She'd known them as long as any kid could know another kid. There were others who'd known them that long, but most of them decided to "un-know" them when they got to high school, when it was totally not cool to know kids like "Shrimpboat" and "Wheezer." Amy didn't care about that. She was fearless when it came to peer pressure. If you wanted to be her friend, you took her the way she came. And she was respected for that because she made no exceptions. She wasn't in any clique, but she somehow managed to cut across them. She wasn't “hot,” she wasn't “fast,” she wasn't rich, and she wasn't “connected.” She was smart, but she wasn't awkward like the so-called “nerd girls.” However, she liked the nerd girls and they liked her because Amy treated them with respect. She had known some of them as long as she'd known Jordy and Mitch. The same with the Goth Girls. Amy had concluded that there was no reason to throw someone overboard simply because they weren't “in” according to someone else. That type of behavior was extremely difficult to sustain in an environment like Woody High (actually, it was difficult to sustain in almost any High School) and especially difficult for a girl. Amy managed to pull it off. But there was a cost. Boys were scared of her. They weren't scared to talk to her, or scared to ask for her advice. But they were scared to hang with her or ask her out. She was smart, cute, and knew her own mind, and she had a strong bullshit detector which she had inherited from her father, and all of that was intimidating to most boys, who inherently sensed that she would see through them. Which, of course, she would. Not that she would do them any harm for it, but they didn't know that. Amy's older sister told her that it would all change in college, and that was okay with Amy because she'd seen enough of Woody's “social circuit” to see through that too. And so it was that Amy Danforth looked at Jordy and Mitch with those red cards in their hands and winced, and felt for them, and genuinely wished she could do something about it. And they knew it. Which was at least something. But this was way beyond her abilities. And they knew that too.

Jordy and Mitch walked forlornly through the school parking lot, toward the waiting black Escalade SUV as the self-proclaimed cool kids snickered derisively, throwing verbal taunts. "Vomit" and "Big-E" were here, along with many other guys and girls. The taunts themselves didn't bother them, not any more – they'd had been called everything, dozens of times, so those arrows bounced off their outer shells. No, it was the dreaded uncertainty of what was to come that ripped them up. No matter what they anticipated, it was always something different. Even when that "something" was milder than expected, the anticipation of the unknown got to them every time. It was a technique well known to torturers, not that they knew that. If they did, it would have only made them feel worse.

Flanking the vehicle were, as always, its owner and driver, Alan "Cold" Winter and, shotgun, Johnny "Deuce" Pullman. Winter's nickname was obvious, even though hardly anyone called him that anymore. For a few months in 5th grade, he was called "The Hulk," but that ended when he beat up the kid who came up with it. After that, it was "Cold," and after that, just "Winter." He was 6 foot 2 and could have easily made the football team, but he didn't feel like playing with a bunch of losers like the Sentinels and, besides, the hours of practice would have cut into his "fun." "Deuce" was so known because he smoked cigarettes – and blunts

– two at a time. And he never was without whatever stuff anyone wanted: he was the supplier. His lanky, 5 foot 10 inch frame also towered over the victims. Deuce never said much, and was totally comfortable doing whatever dirty job he was assigned. The boys knew little about him other than a rumor that he'd been kicked out of several schools before he came to Woody.

Winter pushed back his blond hair and opened the tailgate. "In there, pissfuckers! And don't mess up my firewood!"

The bed of the rear was so covered in firewood that Jordy and Mitch had to sit on top of it. Ouch. They sighed and silently climbed in, using their backpacks to cushion themselves from the sharp edges of the wood. Deuce threw two pillowcases at them. Again, they didn't have to be told what to do: they put them over their heads. Even before the tailgate slammed shut, they heard other cars gunning out of the lot toward... where? That damned uncertainty. Where would it be this time?

***

The ride was three-and-a-half songs long, three-and-a-half thumping, pounding, profanity filled songs by bands they didn't know and didn't care to know, taking them across the railroad tracks and eventually down a rock road that was the music's gravel equivalent. Winter made sure to hit every pothole and bump to remind them they were lying on firewood. And then they stopped.

The tailgate opened and the boys were yanked out of the vehicle and kicked to the ground. The pillowcases were pulled from their heads. They were at the Reeves Road Dump. Again.

"Niles says, *on your knees!*"

It was the voice they most hated to hear in the entire world, announcing another round of his twisted variation of "Simon Says." They got on their knees, on the painful gravel surface, and looked down at the ground as the feet of Doug Niles approached.

"Niles says, *look up!*"

They obeyed and looked up at the sadistic countenance of Douglas K. Niles. Like father, like son, Doug Niles was an asshole. A major asshole. *The* major asshole. He was a charismatic bully – the hot shot with the best car, the best clothes, the most money, the hottest girl, and the most sycophants. Five foot nine, with tight, curly, close-cropped dark hair, and steely blue eyes, he could turn on the charm when he wanted to, usually with teachers and administrators, and they generally bought his bullshit because it was easier and safer – no one in Westover was anxious to have Doug's father as an enemy. And so he got away with it. Even the Seniors gave him a wide berth. Niles hocked loogies on each of their faces. The boys knew not to wipe it off.

"Over here, dickwads, smile for the camera!"

They looked over at Steve "Cam" Cameron, who was never without at least two cameras, recording devices, smartphones, tablets or whatever else was the state-of-the art in technology.

Cam had a lens rig on his left wrist so he could record a second video angle just by pointing his hand. A bit geekier than the others, Cam was The Tech Guy of "The Syndicate" and the computer whiz behind *Hard Woody 411*. Last year, when Niles decided Facebook was for losers, Cam got in his good graces by creating *Hard Woody 411.* Its success made Cam indispensable, despite occasional friction between him and Niles.

Everyone at Woody High logged onto *Hard Woody 411*, but the only way you could post was via direct approval by Niles. Those who were approved were known as the "Hard Corps," and that's who comprised the two dozen or so other spectators here. They formed a semi-circle around Jordy and Mitch, and passed around blunts and booze, as usual. Attendance at a certain number of these "events" was expected – it was how you paid tribute to the king (along with monthly dues), and it was how Niles enforced his power. Woe to anyone who stopped showing up. To stop showing up would be to question the judgment of Niles, and everyone knew the price of that. Similarly, taking and posting photos of the events, or even texting or tweeting about them was absolutely forbidden. Niles and the Syndicate exercised total control over all Syndicate related information and media just like any self-respecting third-world despot.

"I said *smile*, dickwads!" Cam repeated.

As the boys smiled at Cam, they had gravel kicked in their faces, courtesy of the shiniest Prada black leather bitch boots in the school. “I didn't hear anyone say, 'Niles says,' turd boys!” Kellie Davies gave them her most withering stare. Kellie was Niles's girl, the fifth and final member of The Syndicate. She was beautiful, tantalizing, intimidating and superior, a true bitch goddess, in a tight black designer dress that accentuated every curve of her perfect body. In her 3-inch heeled boots, she was an inch taller than Doug. A look from her ice blue eyes could kill. She was, in her own way, as dangerous as Niles – maybe even more dangerous, because Niles listened to her.

“Tell 'em, Doug.”

Niles glared at the boys. “You stool samples are in big trouble: you forgot Kellie's birthday.”

Mitch gulped. “Oh. Happy Birthday, Miss Kellie.”

“My birthday was in March, you little pieces of shit.” She tossed her head dismissively, sending her raven hair off her face.

“Niles says, kiss her boots!”

The boys obeyed, each kissing one of her boot toes.

Then Winter kicked more gravel at them. “It's pretty fucked up that it took you this long to remember it.”

Jordy stuttered. “ We – uh – we never knew about it, actually.”

Niles responded in disbelief. “What the fuck? You mean you never went to the trouble to find out about her birthday? Don't you have any respect at all?”

“Obviously not,” offered Deuce.

"I think I'm being insulted," Kellie said. She leaned over teasingly toward Jordy and Mitch. "What's wrong? Don't you two little baby girls like me?"

"Uh, well, sure, we like you," answered Jordy."

Niles slapped him. "Who gave you permission to like her, Shrimpboat? She's *my* girl. You got the hots for *my girl?*"

Mitch reacted defensively. "No, never, never."

"No, never?" repeated Winter. "Are you saying she's not hot?"

"Only a faggot would think she's not hot," said Niles. "Is that what you're trying to say, Wheezer? That you're a faggot?"

Mitch shook his head. "No..."

Kellie laughed. "Then prove it," she ordered. "Stand up and pull down your pants. Let's see it! Let's see if you're a real man."

Mitch was speechless, frozen in complete disbelief. This was entering a new level of humiliation.

"Niles says, obey Miss Kellie."

"And Miss Kellie says, stand up and drop your pants."

Mitch still hesitated.

Deuce blew cigarette smoke in his face. "Well? She gave you a command, bitch. Whatcha waitin' for?"

"I think he needs some motivation," said Niles. "Winter – give Wheezer some motivation."

Winter grinned as he approached Mitch. Mitch started to choke as he held back an asthma attack, but Winter grabbed Jordy instead, yanked him to his feet and put his arm in a hammerlock.

"Owww!" yelled Jordy.

Winter glared at Mitch. "Pull down your pants, bitch, or I'll break his arm!"

"Okay, okay, don't hurt him! I'll do it! I'm doing it!" He quickly stood up and unbuckled his pants. Cam videoed the whole thing while the Hard Corps whooped it up. Mitch's face turned red as he stood there in his tighty whities.

"The panties too," demanded Kellie. "NOW!"

Winter jerked harder on Jordy's arm. Jordy screamed in pain as his eyes started to tear up. "OWWW!!! Stop! You're breaking my -- OWWW!"

Mitch couldn't bear to see his friend suffering. He had no choice. He pulled down his briefs.

There was laughter from everyone.

Winter laughed loudest as he let up on the hammerlock. "Anybody got a microscope?"

Cam moved in for a closeup. "I'm using the zoom lens and I can barely see it!"

"Maybe it's really a clit!" Deuce suggested.

Niles chortled. "The guy's naked in front of Kellie and it's a shriveled maggot. You're a fag, all right, Wheezer. Might as well admit it. Niles says, *admit it!*"

Cam pointed a lens at his face. "Say it for the cameras, boy. Tell everybody what you are. What are you? Say it!"

The assembled sycophants took up the chant. "*Say it! Say it! Say it!*"

The rhythm built relentlessly as various kids came forward to taunt Mitch. The poor kid was practically crying. Winter snarled at him. "What's wrong, ya need more motivation?" Winter jerked Jordy's arm again. Jordy screamed. Now he really was crying from the pain.

Mitch wheezed and choked out the words. "I -- I'm a f-f-faggot!"

Whoops and hollers rang out from the crowd. But that wasn't enough for Niles. He leaned in toward Mitch. "You're a faggot with a teeny weenie! Niles says, say it!"

Mitch was totally broken. "I'm a faggot with... a teeny weenie!"

There were more catcalls and laughter. Niles turned to Jordy. "And what do we call a cry-baby whose best friend is a faggot?"

Cam turned his lenses on Jordy.

"Say it, cry-baby! Say what you are!" commanded Kellie.

Jordy knew resistance was futile. And dangerous. "I'm a fag, okay? Just stop hurting me! Please! I'm a shrimp fag!"

Winter released him. Jordy fell to the ground.

"I knew it!" shouted Niles triumphantly. "Cam, post it. Let's roll, people!"

Group members high-fived and backslapped Niles for a great show as they headed to their cars. Niles planted a big, wet kiss on

Kellie and they got into his black BMW 5-Series. Winter and Deuce took off in Winter's Escalade, while Cam left solo in his old RAV4. As a parting gesture, “Vomit” and “Big-E” dumped out Jordy's and Mitch's backpacks.

***

The boys waited until everyone was gone. Only then did Mitch put his pants back on. Only then did Jordy repack their backpacks. It was a long walk home, but at least it was over. For today.

Mitch took a hit on his inhaler. Jordy flexed his arm. It hurt, and would probably hurt worse tomorrow.

“It's not broken, is it?” asked Mitch.

“Nah. Hurts like hell though.”

They trudged along the gravel road. Jordy sighed. “Shit, man, how are we gonna survive this year AND next? You ever think about that?”

“Only about 20 times a day.” They walked in silence awhile. “Well,” Mitch offered, “maybe next year there'll be some kids who are more messed up than us and they'll leave us alone.”

“Isn't that we thought *last* year? Besides, that's not gonna solve *this* year. Geez, I wish there was a way out.”

Mitch sighed. “Sometimes at night, before I go to bed, I pray that all five of 'em will, like, get in a major car wreck or something."

"Yeah? I do that sometimes too."

"I wonder if God hears us."

"Nah. I mean, if He did hear us, you'd think He'd do something to make 'em stop. He's not payin' any attention. None."

"But you *do* believe in God, don't you, Jordy?"

"Yeah, I guess. But sometimes it's really hard."

"Maybe it all, like, some big giant test we gotta survive. Like, to toughen us up or something."

"Well, if so, I hope it's over soon, 'cause it totally sucks."

Mitch wheezed again and took another hit from his inhaler. Jordy looked at him sympathetically. Poor kid. To be small, to have no parents, to have asthma and to be a perennial target. What plan exactly did God have in mind for Mitchell Simon?

"Hey, Mitch? Do you ever think about, uh...well, y'know, like, uh...doing yourself?"

"***No!*** I mean, like, if you kill yourself, you automatically go to hell."

"So you still believe in hell?"

"Man, I *gotta* believe in hell. Because if there *is* hell, it means Niles and the Syndicate and all the Hard Corps, they're all gonna end up there. But if there isn't, and there's no heaven and no God, then, like, what's the point, right?"

"I guess."

"Besides, even if there isn't, I couldn't do myself because of

Bagel. I mean, who'd take care of him? I'm all he's got." Bagel was Mitch's beagle and his absolute best friend in the whole world, a gift from his late Grandma Paula, and it was the very best gift he'd ever gotten. Mitch had raised him from a puppy. "What about you, Jordy? You ever think about... doing... *that?*"

Actually, he had. How could he not? Not seriously, but...well, he *had.* But no need for Mitch to know that. Instead, Jordy just smiled. "I wouldn't give Niles the satisfaction." Because that was also true.

The sound of distant thunder came just in time to change the subject. They looked at the western sky. Clouds were rolling in -- dark clouds, threatening clouds. Jordy sniffed the air. He could always smell the ozone that accompanied an approaching lightning storm, and he could smell it now, big time. "Storm's coming," he said. "Major."

"Maybe Niles'll get struck by lightning," said Mitch.

"We wish."

Chapter 3

The storm that night was the biggest in recent memory, at least in terms of lightning and thunder. Mitch knew this because of how frightened Bagel was – he'd never seen the dog so scared. The little beagle was literally shaking, and Mitch held him tightly and stroked his head, speaking calmly and reassuringly. "It's okay, Bagel, I'm here. I'm with you, boy. I'll protect you. Always. I'll never let you down." A huge lightning flash was followed by a thunderclap so powerful, it shook the walls. Bagel whimpered, and Mitch reassured him. "It's just thunder, Bagel. It can't hurt you. It means God's angry. But not with you, Bagel. Never with you."

Mitch lived in a mobile home on the wrong side of the tracks with his mother's sister Sally. The story, as Mitch understood it, was that his party-girl mother, Linda, had gotten pregnant in high school. She ran off and left him behind shortly after he was born. So her mother -- his grandmother Paula -- did the proper, Christian thing, and took him in, to this same mobile home where she lived with her oldest daughter, Sally. Sally was 8 years older than his mother and had never married, due to the combination of her obesity and her less-than-sparkling personality. Linda's behavior permanently destroyed her relationship with Paula and Sally who, as far he knew, had never spoken with “that harlot Linda” again. Mitch had never even seen a picture of his mother, and no one was sure who his father was – there were apparently several candidates. The matter was simply never spoken of. Grandma Paula had never been in the best of health, so when she died nearly five years ago, Sally got to keep the mobile home on the condition that she'd take care of Mitch. Aunt Sally constantly told Mitch she took care of him solely because she was a good Christian, but Mitch knew better because he'd heard the lawyer explain the provisions of the will to Sally after grandma died. Besides, Mitch didn't see a lot of “good Christian behavior” from his aunt, unless you considered watching Reverend Ray Lee Taggart's Worldwide Christian Ministries on TV several hours a day while munching tortilla chips, sitting on your huge ass and collecting welfare to qualify. Or washing his mouth out with soap any time he said anything she found the least bit offensive. Or once referring to him as a “mistake of nature” when she had no idea Mitch was listening.

Normally, Mitch would be doing his homework at Jordy's house. Jordy had a decent computer and internet access, and was always willing to share, while Aunt Sally was suspicious of computers and thought the internet was a tool of the devil, even though her TV Minister had his own website open for donations 24/7. But Mitch wasn't about to ride his bike in a storm like this, especially not with Bagel alongside. So it was homework at home tonight.

The voice of the Reverend Ray Lee Taggart boomed from the living room TV almost as loud as the thunder. "And then God will punish those who revel in their sexual perversions and spread them like a poison across our great land! Men who lie with men! Women who lie with women! Fornication out of wedlock! And those who pollute their holy bodies with the pestilence of drugs! Verily, they will all burn in hell for these repugnant acts, suffering eternal damnation!"

Mitch had heard it all before, often daily. Sometimes he was inclined to believe it and sometimes not so much. He had certainly never heard this sort of message from Pastor Phelps when he went to the Third Congregational Church on Sundays. Pastor Phelps talked of forgiveness and salvation, while Taggart preached hellfire. But unlike Taggart, Pastor Phelps never talked about sex.

Sex. It was a subject that terrified Mitch, a subject to be avoided at all costs. The truth was, sex – or "for-ni-CAY-shun" as Taggart called it – had destroyed his family. Mitch knew he was the product of a "for-ni-CAY-shun" that, according to Taggart, condemned his unknown parents to eternal damnation. So what did that make him? As such a product, could he ever be a decent person? If he was, wouldn't that mean that a godless, unholy act of animal "for-ni-CAY-shun" resulted in something good? And if the result was good, how could the act itself be evil? Did God actually intend for him to be born? Certainly, God *must* have intended it or

Mitch wouldn't be here. It was all so troubling, and it was a lot easier to simply not think too much about any of it. Yet it was hard not to. Why did Niles and the others keep calling him and Jordy fags? Could he be gay and just not know it? He wasn't really interested in girls. But he wasn't interested in boys either. So maybe he wasn't anything. He never talked to Jordy about it. And Jordy never talked to him about it either. It was uncomfortable. Did that mean something? Or nothing? Better to just not think about it. Better to think about something else.

Mitch cuddled Bagel and looked at the pictures of the animals he had taped to his walls. If Mitch could have one wish, it would be to spend his life involved in some way with animals. Dogs. Cats. Horses. Rabbits. Elephants. Even mice. Mitch loved all animals. And animals seemed to love him. Dogs on the street would frequently come over to him for a head scratch or a tummy rub, instinctively sensing that he was a friend. Goats at the petting zoo would always go to him. Sometimes birds would land on his shoulder. So Mitch wished for a future with animals, and dogs were his first choice, because dogs were the best. And yet, he was allergic. Animal hair was bad for his asthma – at least that's what Aunt Sally said. She didn't much like Bagel, and the only reason she put up with him was because of how the pooch centered Mitch. Aunt Sally often said that Mitch's asthma might improve without the dog, but Mitch was firm. He'd rather have asthma and a dog than no asthma and no dog. Still, it just wasn't fair. He had just one dream for his future, and apparently God gave him an allergy to make sure it wouldn't come true. On the other hand, this was all based on what Aunt Sally said. Maybe he wasn't allergic to animal hair. Maybe he was actually allergic to Aunt Sally. That thought made Mitch smile.

Bagel barked softly. Mitch knew what that meant. Bagel always barked a split second before the phone rang, proof again that dogs were the best. And, sure enough, the phone rang.

"Mitchell!" screamed Aunt Sally. "Answer the phone! Can't you see I'm watching TV?"

Mitch silently went into the living area to answer their single land line phone. Mitch had on several occasions tried to convince his aunt that they could afford cell phones through the Life Line Program. Even their Welfare Worker had tried. Mitch argued that he could someday have an asthma attack and would need a cell phone to call for medical attention. But Aunt Sally was convinced that the devil's hand was in almost all modern technology, and she intended to remain pure. Or something.

Mitch knew it was Jordy calling because it was 7:05 and that's when *Hard Woody 411* was usually posted. Mitch took the phone into his room – he had paid for the 50 foot phone wire himself – and shut the door. "So how bad is it?"

"Let's just say you're probably lucky not to have internet access."

Jordy was in his room, with his door closed, looking at his

computer screen where the current edition of *Hard Woody* stared back at him. The headline read, **True Confessions: They're Fags!**

"Am I nude?" asked Mitch.

"Not exactly," Jordy explained. "There's photos of us, and on your crotch is an animated little wet noodle."

"You mean it doesn't actually show it?"

"No. I think if they showed it, it would be child porn and they could go to jail or something. But when you click on our pictures..." Jordy held the phone up to the speaker so Mitch could hear. When he clicked Mitch's image, it played video of Mitch saying, "I'm a – a – f-f-fa-fa-faggot with a teeny weenie." And when he clicked his own image, the video played him saying, "I'm a fag, okay? I'm a shrimp fag."

"Oh, that's harsh. Maybe we should cut tomorrow."

"Are you crazy? We've already got two unexcused absences and it's barely October. Six and we get in major trouble. We might have to repeat the whole year. Me, I'm holding my three in reserve."

"Point. But tomorrow sure ain't gonna be fun."

"Mitch? When has *any* day at school ever been fun?"

"True. Only some have been less fun than others."

"I better do my homework."

"Jordy?" Mitch wheezed as he often did when he was upset or stressed. "Why do they keep doing this to us? Why? Why us?"

"I don't know, Mitch. I don't know. They're just bad. Rotten.

Pieces of shit." Jordy could hear Mitch trying to hold back his tears. "Mitch? Give Bagel a tummy rub from me, okay?"

"Yeah. Okay. See you tomorrow."

Jordy heard Mitch hang up. He knew his best friend was crying, and could only hope Bagel would give him some solace. Too bad there was no one to give him any. His mother was still at work, but even if she'd been home, he couldn't talk to her about this stuff. Cindy Hubbard mostly overreacted, and usually behaved as if whatever was happening to him was actually happening to her. If he told her he was upset, she would become upset that he was upset. If he told her he was angry, she would become angry over whatever was making him angry. Too many times he had tried to talk to her about what he was going through, only to end up having to comfort her because she thought she had failed as a mother. And whenever she tried to fix things, she somehow made them worse. He knew that she meant well, and that she put food on the table, and that, thanks to her, he never really wanted for any important stuff, but it was easier to just say nothing and deal with things himself. And his father? His father was a gutless, irresponsible deadbeat who had left his mother and older sister and him high and dry ten years ago for some bimbo in Florida whom he'd met online. Jordy sighed and wondered about his own future. How would things turn out for him? He had no idea what kind of life he was suited for. He liked computers, but he was no whiz. He liked digging around in junkyards, so maybe something like archeology made sense, although he hardly knew anything about it. Well, at least he didn't have to decide anytime soon. No, right now, he had to worry about tomorrow and next week and next month. He looked up at the posters on his walls. Why couldn't he find a pathway to Middle Earth, get out of Kansas and go on a quest? Why couldn't he turn himself into the Incredible Hulk and pound the bad guys to smithereens? Why couldn't he transfer to Hogwarts? Or why couldn't a space ship come down and take him away from all of this? It just wasn't fair.

***

The storm continued. Mitch dried his eyes again as he killed the light. He climbed into bed and Bagel snuggled in next to him. He looked out the window where lightning was still illuminating the sky. "God, if you're listening, please make 'em stop. Niles and Kellie and Winter and Cam and Deuce. Just make 'em stop. I'll try to be better too, but it'd be a lot easier if I didn't have to worry about those ass-- uh, jerks..."

***

At the exact same moment, a mile and half away, Jordy Hubbard was in his bed, and he too had decided to pray. "...if you don't wanna do it for me, God, do it for Mitch. He can't help it that he was born with asthma. He shouldn't have to suffer more. It's just not right. Those bastards shouldn't be allowed to get away with it. They should all pay. Please help us, God. Thank you."

Simultaneously, both boys said "Amen."

And – call it a coincidence, or fate, or whatever you want – the heavens responded with three massive lightning bolts and sharp, shattering thunderclaps that were so close together that they sounded like one.

Bagel sat up, alarmed. "It's okay, Bagel," said Mitch. "It's just more of the same." But Bagel didn't think so. He cocked his head. He lifted an ear. He sniffed. Mitch wondered what the dog was reacting to. Was it an unusual atmospheric condition? Or something else? "Whaddaya think, Bagel? You think God heard me that time? You think it means something?"

The dog jumped off the bed, trotted over to the window, and looked out. He woofed, agitated, as if something was out there. Mitch looked over at him. "Bagel, it's probably just raccoons. Or possums."

But Mitch was wrong. If he had gone to the window and looked out, he would have seen a figure in a hoodie standing stoically in the downpour, looking intently at the Simon mobile home, oblivious to the rain. Bagel saw him. Or sensed him. And the figure saw – or sensed – Bagel. Bagel then scurried to rejoin Mitch in bed.

Outside, the figure took a few steps sideways, and accidentally kicked the top off of a stubby walkway light fixture. With its cover off, rain got into it. Sparks shot out as it short circuited. The figure looked at the damage, stroked his chin, then squatted, picked up the cover and placed it firmly back where it belonged. He held it there for one second, then two seconds, then three seconds. And then the light came back on. And there was another bolt of lightning, and after that, the figure was gone without a trace. Not even a footprint in the mud.

Chapter 4

They were taunted relentlessly the next morning, on the bus and in the school halls. "Hey, it's wet noodle and mini-fag!" "Any cream sauce on that noodle, Wheezer?" "Teeny pee-pee, he's so cree-pee!" "Shrimpboat's a fa-aag! Shrimpboat's a fa-aag!" These were accompanied by the usual "accidental" body slams into lockers. As usual, the boys suffered in silence. They'd learned long ago that fighting back made it worse, and it was bad enough already.

Amy Danforth had seen the post and felt ashamed, not only for Jordy and Mitch, but for herself because it was another reminder of how powerless she was to do anything about it. That was the hard part of having a moral compass. But like the boys, she suffered in silence because few of her friends cared. To them, the things that happened to the victims of The Syndicate might as well be happening in another Universe, and those things were simply not their concern. It was ignorance as a survival mechanism, but that sort of ignorant bliss did not suit Amy.

***

The new kid showed up in Second Period Algebra. Mr. Tidrow was at the blackboard, explaining how to find "x" by factoring binomials to his disinterested class, a class which included Jordy, Mitch and Alan Winter. The door squeaked open and the new kid entered. And the one word that best described him was *mess.* He was of average height, gangly, with scraggly brown hair that looked like it hadn't been washed in a week. His clothes were ratty and unkempt and didn't seem to fit right, and his bad posture made them look worse. His dirty orange sneakers were untied, and were adorned with an unknown logo of a circle with three hooks coming out of it -- probably knockoffs that came from a swap meet. In fact, his whole look screamed "swap meet." Along with several textbooks, he carried the ugliest DayGlo purple binder that anyone had ever seen. He was greeted by subdued snickers from the class.

Mr. Tidrow eyed him with uncertainty. "Yes? May I help you?"

"Uh, yeah, I guess. I'm, like, new here, and I think I'm, like, supposed to be in this class?"

The new kid reached into his binder to get the transfer slip and somehow managed to drop everything – his books and binder spilled to the floor. So, in addition to being a mess, he was a klutz. The students responded with more snickers as the embarrassed new kid bent down to pick everything up.

Mr. Tidrow looked at the form and read the name. "James

Batt. B-A-T-T. Unusual name. What's the origin?"

The new kid stood up, not quite understanding. "Huh? The what?"

"The origin. The origination. Where did your name come from?"

"Oh. It was my father's."

There was chortling from the class. The new kid was a mess, a klutz *and* he was clueless. Jordy and Mitch exchanged a look of disbelief.

Mr. Tidrow rifled through some papers on his desk, then shook his head. "Your transfer slip is correct, but I don't have any paperwork work on you, Mr. Batt."

"So you want me to leave?"

"No, take any open seat. I'm sure it'll get sorted out soon enough." Mr. Tidrow addressed the class. "Everyone? This is James Batt. Please make him feel welcome." He again turned to the newcomer. "Do they call you James or Jim?"

"Uh, well, actually, my friends call me J.B."

"How about Batt-man?" shouted Winter. The class's laughter encouraged him. "Yo, we got Batt-man in our class! Hey, you got a Batmobile, Batt-man?"

"Huh? Oh, you mean, like, a car? Uh, no."

"Like I care."

"That's enough, Mr. Winter. Let's get back to our problem, please."

Mr. Tidrow turned back to the display board to factor the equation. As Batt walked down the aisle toward an empty desk, Winter stuck his foot out and tripped him. Batt hit the floor, and his books went flying. Everyone could now see that Batt had one white sock and one black.

Winter couldn't resist. “Nice socks, Batt-man! And I'll bet you got another pair just like it at home!”

Mr. Tidrow turned around, unaware that Batt was tripped. “Perhaps, Mr. Batt, if you tied your shoes, you wouldn't trip over yourself.”

“Yes, sir,” mumbled Batt as he took a seat.

Again Mitch and Jordy traded a look. The new kid was off to a very bad start.

***

The lunchroom at Woody High was, like most school lunchrooms, a collection of segregated enclaves. Every clique had a table or part of a table, and everyone sat where they belonged. These were, among others: the Jocks. The Student Council. The Fast Girls. The Computer Geeks. The Goths. The Black Militants. The Nerd Girls. The Wallflower Girls. The Musicians. The Skaters. The Artsies. The ethnic Mexicans. The ethnic Hondurans. The Dopers. The Syndicate had their table. And those without a clique, which included Jordy and Mitch, sat at one of several "exile" tables, all at the same place every day.

James Batt stepped out of the food line carrying a tray with something the school called "pasta," a soft roll, a glass of milk, and a dessert resembling chocolate cake. He surveyed the tables, trying to get the lay of the land. And then he heard a familiar voice.

"Hey, Batt-man! Over here!"

It was Winter, calling him over to the Syndicate's table. Batt looked over that way. "C'mon, Batt-man! No hard feelings. Come on over and meet my guys."

Batt shrugged and went over there. Some six tables away, Mitch and Jordy saw what was happening. The hazing was about to begin.

Niles, Deuce, Cam and Kellie all gave him the once over, like hungry jackals eying a lone antelope.

"Guys," said Winter, "meet Batt-man."

"Hey," said Batt, nodding.

"Where's your cape, Batt-man?" cackled Deuce.

Batt cleared his throat. "It's, uh, J.B. My friends call me J.B."

Niles slammed a fist on the table. "Yeah, well, we ain't your friends, dickhead. Not yet. Maybe not ever. But if Alan Winter says your name's Batt-man, then your name's Batt-man, understand?"

"Sorry, guess I'm at the wrong table," Batt replied, trying to save face as he took a few steps backward.

But Niles was just getting started. “Hey, where ya goin', Batt-man? Nobody said you could leave. Sit down. That is, if you wanna survive.”

Batt looked at him – at the cold stare, the expensive clothes, and the Rolex watch. He knew the type. Batt took a deep breath and sat down. He was tense. He'd been here before.

“Good. You understand English. We just might get along. I'm Doug Niles. I call the shots around here. And if I don't like you, well, let's just say "shit happens." And so far, I don't like you. I don't like your face, I don't like your clothes, I don't like your fucking name. So tell me, Batt-man, you got any money?”

“Shit, Doug,” said Cam, “can't you see he spends it all on his wardrobe!”

Batt cleared his throat. “No, I don't have any money.”

“Too bad,” said Niles. “That means you don't get to eat today. Unless you don't mind eating off the floor, on your hands and knees.”

Niles gave Deuce a nod and Deuce dumped Batt's tray of food and his books on the floor.

The sound of the impact got everyone's attention, including Mr. Cutler, the handsome 30-year old sandy-haired school counselor who was a lunch room monitor this term. Half the girls in school had a crush on him. He came over to the scene of the mess, took it all in and looked at Niles knowingly.

“Mr. Niles, do we have a problem?”

“No, sir. Just a slight accident, that's all. No harm, no foul.”

Mr. Cutler looked at the new kid sympathetically. “Son, is there a problem? You can tell me the truth.”

Batt hesitated. They were all staring at him. He took a deep breath. He knew the drill. “No, sir. No problem, sir. It was my fault.”

“You're sure?”

“Yes, sir.”

Mr. Cutler nodded, then wandered off.

Kellie looked at the others. “He's smarter than he looks.”

Niles turned to Batt. “Life lesson, Batt-man: The weak and the poor will always be oppressed by the rich and powerful. The only variable is the degree of oppression. And that's entirely up to you. Understand?”

Batt lowered his head. “Yeah.”

“Good. See you after school. West parking lot. Consider this an 'invitation.' You're gonna be the lead story in *Hard Woody 411*. And if you don't know what I mean, you got till 3 o'clock to find out. Now, quit polluting my eyesight, quit breathing my air, and fuck off.”

Batt picked up his books and his binder and sauntered away with a posture of utter defeat.

Niles and company chortled.

***

Mitch turned to Jordy with cautious amazement. “Maybe our prayers got answered! They got somebody new to pick on!”

Jordy nodded. “They sure do.”

***

Batt wandered around, looking for a place to sit. He spotted the empty spaces next to Jordy and Mitch and headed that way. But Jordy and Mitch wanted nothing to do with him. They looked away, and sent the message with their body language.

Batt got it, and walked right past them. Jordy and Mitch sighed relief, then watched as Batt shuffled along, table to table.

The Shop Kids threw trash at him.

A clique of girls responded with coughing and gagging.

The Skaters sprayed soda at him.

The Jocks hocked loogies at him.

Jordy and Mitch watched with pained expressions. They'd been there, more than once. They asked the question with traded looks: should we? Jordy shrugged, noncommittal, but Mitch had empathy.

So when Batt glanced over at them again, Mitch gave him a nod. Batt came over again and sat down. “Hey,” he said quietly.

“Hey,” replied Mitch.

“Welcome to Woody High,” said Jordy.

"I'm J.B."

"Not today," said Jordy. "Today you're 'on the menu.' Today you're 'fresh fish.'"

Batt sighed and nodded. "Yeah. Shit, it's always the same. Every fucking school. I'm "Batt Man" or "Batt Brain" or "Batt Shit." How do you guys put up with it?"

"Well," said Mitch, we just --"

Jordy cut him off. "How do you know we put up with anything?"

Batt looked at them and smiled. "When you been to as many schools as I have, you always know. Who the victims are."

Mitch and Jordy traded a look. Busted.

"It's that obvious, huh?" asked Jordy.

"Yep."

"Well," said Mitch, "the deal around here is, Niles and those guys are terrorists. They call themselves "The Syndicate." And everybody gives 'em a pass. Including the teachers."

"What, Niles's old man got some pull?"

Jordy nodded. "Rich lawyer. School doesn't want any legal problems. Here, have some of my grapes."

Batt nodded his thanks and took a bunch. "So who's the hard core? Niles and those three guys?"

"And his girl. Kellie," added Mitch. "Always giving him ideas. She's mean. Evil."

"Be afraid," said Jordy. "Be very afraid."

“No shit?” As they talked, Batt took a pencil from his notebook and stood it upright on its eraser. Then he took another one and did it again.

Jordy explained. “Last year, this girl, Dana Madison, started saying Kellie was, like, y’know, doing it for money? Like, hooking? 'Cause she always had lotsa cash and this credit card with some guy's name on it nobody ever head of. Well, Kellie declared Dana a non-person, said she "didn't exist." And she got everyone on board 'cause no one wanted cross her or The Syndicate. So that's what happened. No one talked to her, no one acknowledged her, everyone talked trash about her, I mean, it was cold. They made her life hell. She was always crying, she got fat, her grades hit the toilet. Finally she tries to kill herself. Fails. But at least her parents knew enough to get her outta here. They tried to sue the school because Kellie had posted the "rules" about Dana on the internet. They said the school shoulda stopped it, but the school said they weren't responsible because it wasn't their website, and they couldn't force kids to be nice to each other. So that gave Kellie and Niles permission to run their Hate Site. "Hard Woody 411."

“It's cruel,” said Mitch.

Batt set up a 4th pencil. “So why won't someone fight fire with fire? Do the same thing to them?”

Jordy shrugged. “Takes time, money, and technology. And guts. Easier to just steer clear.”

“Okay, then what about when they go after the minority kids and use, like, the n-word? Then it would be, like, racist hate speech.”

“Yeah, but they leave them alone,” Jordy explained. “They never harass the blacks or the Hispanics or the Asians. It's like they know not to. And, like, last night? They posted this nude photo of Mitch, but they put a cartoon noodle over his dick so that it wouldn't be kiddie porn. They've never actually shown any girl's nipples either. Sometimes I think Niles's old man told 'em what they could and couldn't get away with.”

“Wow, that's really fucked up.” Batt looked back toward The Syndicate's table. “So is Kellie really, like, a teenage hooker?”

Mitch answered quickly. “As far as we're concerned, she's the nicest girl in school. So even if she rips you, thank her for acknowledging your existence.”

Batt nodded. “So it's four guys and a girl this time. Five.” He set up pencil number five, five vertical pencils, all in a row. And then knocked number five over into the others: they all went down like dominoes.

“One more thing,” said Mitch. “You'll probably get "invited" to appear in Hard Woody 411.”

“Already did. Today after school.”

Jordy picked up one of Batt's pencils and tried to stand it on its eraser, but it fell over. He kept trying and failing as Mitch continued.

“Well, avoiding it'll just make it worse. See that kid with the face thing?” He pointed to a kid two tables away wearing a jaw alignment brace. “Dennis Palarin. He avoided it. Never showed up when they told him. Two weeks later, they jumped him in P.E. and broke his jaw. We're talking almost the whole class. A week in the hospital, two surgeries and he still has to wear that brace until who knows when. Maybe, like, forever. Officially it was, quote, 'just some rambunctious boys roughhousing' unquote. Oh, by the way, I'm Mitch, and he's Jordy.”

The boys gave each other mutual nods.

“So, Jordy, Mitch: I got one more question. Do you believe God answers prayers?”

Jordy and Mitch traded another look – an uncomfortable one. They looked back at Batt who studied them intently.

“What are you, like, a Jesus freak or something?” asked Jordy.

“Nope. Just curious if you thought praying did any good. You *do* pray, don’t you?”

Again, Mitch and Jordy looked at each other.

“Yeah,” said Mitch. “But I, uh, haven't decided if it does any good yet.”

“Me neither,” added Jordy.

Batt gathered his books and stood. “I figure you guys'll get a break for a few days. "Fish" is always more appetizing when it's fresh. See ya.”

He walked away, leaving Mitch and Jordy wondering, *who is this guy?*

Chapter 5

Batt shuffled down the hall toward the stairwell, trying to figure out where his 5th period class was. Amy Danforth came up alongside him.

"Hello," she said. "I'm Amy Danforth."

Batt could care less. "Uh huh..."

"They call you J.B., is that right?"

"Uh huh."

"So J.B., whenever somebody new comes here, I do a profile of 'em for the school website. Where you're from, your interests, stuff like that. Helps everyone get to know you."

"No, thanks."

She looked at him with interest. He was a mess, but with some better grooming and better clothes, he could be a decent looking guy. "Oh, don't be so shy, J.B. It'll help you make friends."

"No, I just like to be left alone."

"Really? C'mon, everybody needs friends. Especially the new kid."

Suddenly, Kellie was there with her three-girl entourage, girls who were every bit as hot and fashion savvy as Kellie.

"Actually, Amy, Batt-man's not gonna have any friends. At least not any that matter. We've decided."

"Interesting. So, does J.B. know that?"

"J.B.? Who's J.B.? I don't see anybody named J.B." Kellie looked directly at Batt. "Batt-man, do you see anybody here named J.B?"

Batt looked away from her, but Kellie grabbed his chin – hard -- and turned his face toward hers. "I'm talking to you, Batt-man. Or is it Batt-*girl?* Now answer me! Do! You! See! Anyone! Here! Named! J! B!?"

Batt mumbled softly. "Uh...no."

"No, *what*, ass-wipe?"

"No, I don't see anyone here named J.B., Kellie."

"*Miss* Kellie, to you. That's the way slaves addressed their owners before the Civil War. *Understand*?"

"Yeah."

Her eyes flashed in anger. "Then *say it*, bitch!"

Batt dropped his head in defeat. "Yes, Miss Kellie, I understand."

There were giggles and snickers from Kellie's girls, and from some of the other kids in the hall. Amy cringed.

Kellie, quite pleased with herself, addressed Amy smugly. "He learns quickly, Amy. Maybe you could learn something from him too."

Amy smiled icily. "Thank you, Kellie, I believe you've

already broadened my education significantly in these wonderful and delightful moments we've just spent together."

Kellie's smile was equally frigid. "Always happy to be of service." She turned her attention back to Batt and shoved her armload of books into his chest. "Now carry my books, slave Batt-boy. Upstairs."

"Uh, yeah, but my next class is – "

She kicked his leg out from under him and he hit the floor.

"I don't give a fuck about your next class! Your job is to give a fuck about MY next class! And in case you're wondering, Doug doesn't like it when boys are rude to me. Want me to tell him you were rude to me?"

"No, Miss Kellie."

"Then pick your sorry ass up off the floor and carry my books upstairs."

Batt gathered the books and got back on his feet as Kellie turned back to Amy.

"Oh, Amy, you won't be writing about this little incident on your blog, will you?"

"What incident, 'Miss Kellie?'"

If there had been grass in the hall, it would have iced over with frost.

Kellie smiled. "Excellent answer. Nice to see that you *are* paying attention." She glared at Batt. "Walk behind us, understand, slave?"

"Yes, Miss Kellie."

"And if me or my friends think you're staring at our asses, we'll kick your balls into the middle of next week. Although you might actually like that."

"Yes, Miss Kellie."

She and her girls headed upstairs triumphantly, with Batt trailing meekly along, burdened down with books.

Amy watched him go with a curious expression. Something about him didn't quite make sense, almost as if his behavior had been an act. Maybe it was the way he moved. Maybe it was something in his eyes. Or maybe it was that strange bit of energy she felt when she'd stood next to him. Whatever it was, it triggered something inside her. Her intuition told her there was a mystery here, and mysteries needed to be solved.

Mitch and Jordy had seen most of this too. They shook their heads in complete disbelief. "I didn't think it was possible to be *that* much of a wimp."

"Maybe he likes it or something," said Mitch.

"Or something."

Amy spotted them across the hall, and they all exchanged similar silent reactions.

***

For Jordy and Mitch, the rest of the day was a lot easier

knowing that they would not find a red card in their lockers at 3 o'clock. Moreover, even though Jordy wasn't one of the Syndicate's Twitter followers, he knew the word had been passed around that Woody High had a brand new target. As a result, the harassment they'd received that morning mostly vanished. The boys hadn't had such a stress free afternoon since the last time Niles had been absent.

As they walked toward the school bus at 3:10, they saw a lot of kids milling around in the west parking lot. No doubt, every single one of The Syndicate's Hard Corps was there for Batt's official "initiation." They picked up snippets of conversation.

"...heard Kellie was gonna beat his balls bloody." "Maybe with a bat, 'cause he's Batt-man." "I heard they're gonna take him out to eat." "You mean, like, to a restaurant?" "Maybe make him eat, like 20 jalapenos." "Off the floor." "Maybe make him take his clothes off inside."

Some of the kids thought this stuff was funny. Mitch and Jordy did not. As they took their seats near the back, they looked out and saw Winter's black Escalade pulling out.

"At least it's not us," said Jordy.

"Yeah, but I still feel bad," said Mitch. "I mean, I prayed they'd pick on somebody else, then *he* shows up, and it's like he's suffering because of what I prayed for."

"C'mon, you don't really believe that God answered our prayers?"

Mitch shrugged. "I dunno. Maybe."

"Look, we get, like, one new kid a month. This time he's a wimp. It was bound to happen eventually."

"Okay, but, I still feel bad for him."

"Well, me too. But it's not like we can *do* anything. What, now you're gonna pray that he goes away?"

"No," said Mitch. "Just that they don't hurt him."

Chapter 6

Mitch was having trouble concentrating on his Algebra homework. Algebra made him think of J.B., and that made him worry about the awful things The Syndicate might have done to him. Thus, even when Niles and Company weren't directly harassing him, they were still making his life miserable. Then, for the 26th time, he tried – and failed -- to stand a pencil up on its eraser.

Mitch petted Bagel and sighed. "I'm gonna call him, Bagel. I'm gonna find his number and call him. I mean, like, this is when he totally needs a friend."

As usual, Aunt Sally was watching Reverend Taggart. Mitch quietly walked to the phone and took it to his room. He punched 4-1-1, went through the menus, and finally got a live human being.

"For Westover, Kansas, please. I need a home number for Batt, B-a-t-t. I don't have a first name, but it'll be a new listing."

"I'm sorry," said the operator. "I have no listing under that name, new or old."

Mitch hung up. Okay, not the weirdest thing. Maybe the phone company hadn't installed their phone yet. Maybe they only had a cell phone. Maybe his mother had a different last name. It was 6:45, and it wouldn't be posted before 7. But Mitch couldn't stay in his room wondering all by himself.

"Aunt Sally? Bagel and I are going to Jordy's."

She didn't even look at him. "Be home by nine."

"Yes, ma'am."

Mitch put Bagel in his bike basket and pedaled to Jordy's house. At least Bagel was happy. Like most dogs, the beagle loved the sensation of speed and wind. When he was on his bike with Bagel, Mitch often thought of Dorothy and Toto riding to escape Miss Gulch. Or of Elliot and E.T. Too bad his bike wouldn't levitate.

***

Jordy lived in a small tract house in a subdivision that was built 30 or 40 years ago. Jordy was used to having Mitch show up unannounced. His mom usually didn't get home from work until after eight and his older sister was generally hanging with her junior college friends, so he was happy to have some company. And his mom, who worked two jobs, was never upset about it – on the contrary, she was happy to know that her son wasn't alone. She even got Bagel a dog toy now and then. Mitch had told him many times that he wished his Aunt Sally was as nice to him and Bagel as Jordy's mom was.

Mitch was agitated. "C'mon, Jordy, you can admit it. You're

worried about him too."

"Yeah, sure I am. But, look, it's not like J.B. ignored the invitation. So they're not, like, gonna break his jaw or anything. I mean, what's up, Mitch? You're never like this when they go after other kids."

Mitch sighed. "I know. But I never prayed for bad things to happen to them. And I prayed for this."

"Okay, but you've prayed for it every day and every night for at least a year, right? And all those times, God didn't do a thing about it, right? So why now? Why all of the sudden would God decide to answer your prayers after ignoring 'em for so long?"

"I dunno. Maybe He got tired of me nagging him about it."

"I'll tell you why. *Because He didn't.* Because it's just a coincidence, like I said before."

"J.B. asked us if we prayed, Jordy. Nobody's ever asked me that. Not like that. I think that's a little, y'know, strange. Don't you?"

"Lots of people pray. Especially people in trouble. There's nothin' strange about it at all."

Mitch looked at the clock: 7:06. "It's time, right?"

Jordy logged on to *Hard Woody 411*. They both stared as the screen loaded. And in unison, they both said "Ewww, gross!"

The headline: **NEW KID EATS DOGSHIT ON A BUN AND SAYS YUM-YUM!**

Jordy hesitated, then gave in to his lesser angels – or perhaps it was the little devil on his shoulder -- and clicked on the accompanying picture. It played a video clip that left nothing to the imagination. Mitch coughed and wheezed. He couldn't watch it. And Jordy wished he hadn't.

And if they had been flies on the wall in Amy Danforth's bedroom, they would have seen her reacting in exactly the same way.

***

At school the next morning, Jordy and Mitch spotted Batt coming down the hall in a familiar variation of what they'd endured yesterday morning – and many mornings before. Batt was taunted by guys displaying their witty maturity and was "accidentally" body-slammed as he made his way to his locker.

"Hungry, Batt-man?" "What'd ya have for breakfast, Batt-man?" "Hey, I'm preparing a real nice meal for ya, Batt-man!" "Want some homemade brownies, Batt-man?"

Jordy and Mitch caught up with him. "You all right, J.B.?" asked Jordy.

Batt shrugged. "Would *you* be?"

The taunting continued. "What's for lunch, Batt-man? Hot shit on rye, or cold shit on toast with a diarrhea shake?" "How'd you like some soft serve, Batt-man?"

Mitch asked, "Did you fight back or anything?"

"No," Batt replied. "I'd rather go home and throw up than go to the emergency room all bloody with busted bones. Buncha guys start beatin' on you, it can get *way* outta control. I *know.*"

Jordy and Mitch traded a look. Clearly something *very* bad had happened to this kid.

Mitch stammered. "I, uh, tried to call you last night but I couldn't find your number."

"Yeah, well, I don't want it to be too easy for people to find me, if you know what I mean. No texts, no email, no Facebook. It's safer." With that, he hurried off by himself, trying to ignore the continued verbal pelting that followed him.

***

Jordy and Mitch sat at their usual spot in the lunchroom.

"What if they try to make *us* eat it?" asked Mitch.

Jordy didn't want to think about it, but he couldn't *not* think about it either. "I dunno, man. I dunno. But I guess it *is* better than having a broken jaw."

Batt joined them. He had no tray, no brown bag, and no lunch -- just his trademark purple binder. "Hey."

"No lunch?" asked Mitch.

"Not hungry." *Duh.*

A jerk from the football team came by. "There's fudge for dessert, Batt-man!"

Jordy looked at Batt seriously. "So guys put you in the hospital?"

"Yeah. In Trenton, New Jersey. It was bad."

"What happened?" asked Mitch.

"Three of 'em ambushed me. I fought back, they didn't like it. They shanked me, too. The pain, man. The fucking pain. It was like I died. Like I fucking died."

There was a moment of silence. Finally, Jordy cleared his throat.

"So...tell us something, J.B. Do *you* believe God answers prayers?"

"Me? Yeah. Well – sometimes..." Batt took a deep breath, looked around, then looked back at Jordy and Mitch with the barest hint of a smile. "And sometimes the Devil does."

Jordy and Mitch exchanged a quizzical look.

Then a kid walked by and dropped a red card in front of Batt, and he was gone before anyone could figure out who he was. This red card was little different than the usual "invitations." It said: "You're Invited. Private Event."

Batt showed it to Mitch and Jordy. "Private Event. Is that good or bad?"

"It's always bad," said Jordy. "Public or Private."

Batt dropped his head in his hands and sighed.

***

The "Private Events" were usually attended only by the five core members, and they were private for three main reasons. Reason Number One was to build interest and anticipation from the Hard Corps, and everyone else. After all, one key to being an elite, exclusive group was that attendance at certain events must be restricted. There were times Niles wanted to totally control the flow of information – he didn't like it when word got out about what happened before *Hard Woody 411* was posted. It was important to keep reminding everyone that *he* was the king. Reason Number Two was that Kellie didn't always like having twenty or thirty people around. Truth be told, there were kids in the Hard Corps that she couldn't stand. And besides, her influence on Doug was stronger when there were fewer kids around. And Reason Number Three was that they sometimes went to places that weren't conducive to having a whole bunch of kids show up in their cars.

The Westover Cemetery was such a place. One look at the ramshackle entry gate made it clear that this was definitely not a tourist attraction. But they didn't enter that way. There was another way in, around the back, and not easily noticeable. A rough gravel road took them into the premises. The graveyard was overgrown, and numerous tombstones were overturned. If there actually was a caretaker, no one had ever seen him. Usually the "invited guests" were creeped out by being in a graveyard, which made them more compliant and easier to fuck with. That made it a perfect place for a "private event."

As Batt was dragged out of Winter's Escalade, Cam started recording, narrating as if he were doing a piece on *60 Minutes*. "Welcome to another edition of Hard Woody 411, with our guest, the new kid, known as Batt-man."

Niles stepped over to Batt and poked him in the chest. "I think we figured out your secret, Batt-man. You're a faggot. A real man wouldn't let himself get pushed around like you do. I say you're nothing but a shit-eating, fudgepacking, knob jockey. What do you say?"

Batt stood there stoically and said nothing.

Niles poked him again, harder. "What, are you, deaf? I said you're a faggot! A brownie king! A knob ferret! What do you say?"

Still, Batt was silent.

Niles got right in his face. "Niles says, *answer the question!*"

Batt gulped, looked at his tormentors, and sighed. "You're right."

It was the answer Niles least expected. "Huh? What?"

Batt struck an effeminate, limp-wristed pose and spoke with an exaggerated, higher pitched lisp. "Oh, who needs the closet anyway? I knew I couldn't fool a buncha smart boys like you for very long. Truth is, I'm as queer as a three dollar bill. Why hide it? I'm Queen Batt."

They were all stunned.

Batt wasn't finished, not by a long shot. “So? Who wants a blow job?” He turned to Winter. “I bet you've got a real nice package, tiger.” Then he addressed Cam. “And you, you sexy cameraman, you. I’d love to touch *your* junk. How about you all run a train on me?” Batt swiveled his hips, stuck out his tongue and made some lewd gestures.

The boys were all taken aback. This had *never* happened!

Winter balled his right hand into a fist. “You motherfuckin' pervert!” He decked Batt in the jaw. Batt went down. Blood trickled from his mouth as he lay there.

“Oh, that hurt so good! So good! Could you do that again, please, you big strong hunk of manly man?”

“Ya hear that?” said Winter. “He wants more! Fuckin' A, I'll give you more, faggot!” Winter kicked him in the gut.

Batt groaned with pleasure. “Harder! Do me harder, please! In my balls!”

“You got it, fag boy!” Winter kicked him hard in the nuts.

Batt squealed.

Niles yanked Winter away from Batt. “Stop!” he ordered. “Pick the fag up.”

Winter and Deuce pulled Batt to his feet. Niles faced him. “You're not only a queer, you're a masochist, aren't you?”

Batt shrugged, then puckered his lips.

Winter whispered to Deuce. “What's that mean?”

"You're an idiot," Deuce told him.

"I knew it," continued Niles. "You actually *like* this. Man, you're one sick, limp-wristed fuck. I'll bet you liked that shit sandwich, too."

Batt answered prissily. "Don't knock it if you've never tried it. Although wheat bread, sprouts and a little mayonnaise would have made it much more flavorful."

Niles backhanded him hard across the face.

Batt spit up more blood, then moaned with pleasure. "Mmmmm. That was *so* stimulating! I think I'm in love! Miss Kellie, mind if I steal your boyfriend?"

Niles was pissed. He let loose a stream of profanity and epithets that would make a truck driver blush and then slapped Batt again.

"Thank you, Dougie. I hope it was good for you, too!"

Niles got ready to really whale on him – but suddenly had a change of heart and held back.

Winter cackled sadistically. "It's cool, man! Everybody wins! Let's stomp the son of a bitch!"

Niles turned and glared at Winter. "Shut up! That's *exactly* what he wants! Well, I say, *fuck that*! No sick, limp-wristed faggot is gonna tell me what to do!" Niles put his face closer to Batt's and spoke quietly. "You ever hear the story about the masochist and the sadist, Batt-man? Masochist goes up to the sadist and says, 'Since you're a sadist, will you hurt me? Will you please, please, hurt me?' And the sadist looks at him, smiles, and says... *No*."

Batt reacted with concern.

Winter looked at the others. "I don't get it."

"You're too stupid to live," Kellie told him.

Niles leered at Batt, simmering with hate. *How dare this sissy-boy ruin the plans he'd devised for today.* "Your sick fun's over, stool. You're not using us to get off ever again. We won't give you the satisfaction. From now on, <u>you</u> <u>don't</u> <u>exist</u>. Nobody talks to you, touches you, kicks you -- nobody even acknowledges that you're taking up fucking space."

Batt shook his head in disbelief. "But that's so *mean*! It's *cruel*! I mean, I was really starting to enjoy myself! We were all getting along so well!"

Niles turned to the group. "All right, we're done with this sicko. Nobody says anything about what just happened here. Subject of today's edition: Motherfuckin' Batt-boy doesn't exist. Besides, the two runts are more fun to fuck with. At least they cry."

They all walked away from Batt, toward their cars. Kellie sidled up to Niles. "Hey, Doug, let's have a little party Friday night. Do something special. At *The Cabin*?"

Niles grinned. "Great idea, baby. Great idea."

Batt watched them go, a knowing expression on his face. And when they were gone, he rubbed his hand across his bloody mouth and *the blood vanished.* There was no cut, no wound, no mark, not even blood on his hand.

***

At a few minutes after 7, Amy Danforth, like almost every kid at Woody High, logged onto *Hard Woody 411* in the privacy of her bedroom. Amy did this with a mixture of curiosity and shame. What was the expression? *Like watching an automobile accident.* You don't really want to look, and you know it's not really going to do you any good to look, but you can't *not* look. Amy hated the fact that The Syndicate had this power over her, this power to appeal to her worst instincts. She could rationalize it, and often did: she needed to know what was going on at school. In fact, it was her responsibility to know, because she was a major contributor to the school's website. But there wasn't an evening that went by that she didn't feel a moment of dread and an ache in her stomach when the page loaded onto her MacBook. And on those evenings when she knew the victims, it was worse. She clicked her mouse, and there was the headline: **"THIS PERVERT DOES NOT EXIST!"** It was accompanied by an image of James Batt lying on the ground, next to a tombstone. She clicked on the image. No video, no audio. The accompanying text said nothing about what had happened. It simply stated the "rules" of how "Batt-man" was to be treated from now on. She shook her head sadly. “You never even got a chance.”

***

A similar tableau played out in front of Jordy's computer, as Jordy and Mitch reacted similarly. “Whoa, that didn't take long.” But unlike Amy, they knew they could – and would – find out from J.B. what happened, even if “he didn't exist.” As the lowest bottom feeders in the Woody High food chain, they could pretend a certain amount of ignorance and get away with it, at least for a little while.

***

It was a vastly different experience for Batt as he walked down the hall the next morning. No taunts. No body slams. Nothing thrown at him. No eye contact. Whenever he looked at anyone, they looked away. He heard a couple of comments: “Do you smell dogshit?” asked one kid. “Smells more like puke to me,” was the response. As far as Batt was concerned, his life had greatly improved. He got to his locker in safety. He was going to have a very peaceful Thursday.

***

In the lunchroom, Batt sat with Jordy and Mitch. They reacted with astonishment when he told them what had happened.

“Y'mean they just stopped everything and walked away?” asked Mitch.

“I know, right? I mean, like, they told me I didn't exist, and that was it. Today – all peace and quiet.”

“Whoa,” said Jordy, “I never thought that "turn the other cheek" stuff ever worked.”

“I don't think it's exactly what Jesus had in mind,” said Batt. “The bad news is, they'll be back to kicking your asses again. But just wait until Monday...”

“Monday?” asked Jordy. “What's gonna happen Monday?”

But before Batt could answer, Deuce came over and addressed Jordy and Mitch. “Maybe you stool samples haven't heard, but Batt-man don't exist any more. Understand?”

Mitch gulped and smiled weakly. “Oh, hey, me and Jordy were just sitting here all by ourselves. We don't know nothin' about any Batt-man.”

“Yeah,” agreed Jordy. “Unless you mean, like, y'know, Bruce Wayne. Heh.”

Deuce's eyes narrowed threateningly. “See that you remember it. Because things *can* get uglier. For all concerned.” He walked away.

Jordy and Mitch then talked quietly out of the sides of their mouths without looking at Batt.

"Sorry, J.B., we got no choice here," mumbled Jordy.

"Yeah," Mitch continued. "They're gonna be watchin' us.

Batt stood up. "Then I'll make it easy for you." And he walked away.

Mitch sighed. "And just when I was starting to like that guy. How much do you think he can take?"

"A lot more than we can. A whole lot more."

***

At 3 o'clock, Mitch and Jordy approached their lockers with dread. Given J.B.'s warning, they expected to see red cards. But wonder of wonders, they were wrong.

As they headed out the front doors, Amy joined them.

"So what'd J.B. do to get 'the treatment?'" she asked.

"No comment, Amy," replied Jordy.

"Please. Tell me."

"Why? Why do you care?"

"I don't know exactly, but there's just something about him I find...intriguing."

Mitch gave her a look. "I'll tell you what he did. He was born."

"C'mon, guys," she pleaded, "what *really* happened?"

Jordy nudged Mitch. They were being monitored by Lexi, one of Kellie's posse, who pretended to be talking on her phone as she tailed them.

Mitch spoke a little louder. “Amy, there's nobody I ever heard of that got any 'treatments.'”

“My uncle,” said Jordy. “He got radiation treatments for his cancer. But please don't ask again. It's a very painful subject.”

Amy spotted Lexi and got the message. “Right, I understand.”

The boys hurried off and boarded for their bus, leaving her behind.

“So, Mitch – are you still praying?”

“No. I'm scared to, actually. I haven't prayed since that night.”

“Me neither.”

Further away, stood the solitary figure of James Batt. He stood tall, arms folded, legs apart like a western gunfighter, and watched the school bus drive off. He had the barest hint of a smile on his face.

“Monday, boys,” whispered Batt. “That's when the fun begins. Just hang in 'til Monday.”

Chapter 7

Thursday evening came and went without a new edition of *Hard Woody 411*. Not that there was anything unusual about that – there had been weeks with only one or two postings. And it was rare that there was ever a posting on the weekend. Still, Mitch and Jordy were on edge about everything, particularly because of J.B.'s warning. Had J.B. just assumed The Syndicate would go back to picking on them? Or had he heard them say something? The boys considered every permutation, both together and singly. They couldn't ask J.B. at school because that would incur the wrath of The Syndicate. And they had no way to contact him. Once again, not knowing was torture.

***

Amy was also bothered by not knowing. She really wanted to know what had happened to make J.B. a non-entity. But *why* did she want to know? None of her friends cared. Not one of them was talking or tweeting or texting about it. So why did she care? Was it because she was the only one of her circle who had actually tried to talk to him – and therefore actually thought of him as a human being? Was it because of something she'd seen in his eyes – that he'd clearly been hurt in the past? Or was it because of the injustice of it all – that a kid could come to school, do nothing at all, and suddenly have his life ruined simply because some self-proclaimed cool kids decreed it? It was just so wrong. She thought about calling Jordy. She *knew* that he knew. But would he tell her? Probably not without a lot of effort on her part. It wasn't like they were friends. Not that there were any incidents in the past, or anything – they just traveled in different circles. She knew Jordy had nothing to gain by telling her any secrets, but he had a lot to lose. So she didn't call him.

***

And then it was Friday, and the school day passed, and J.B. was ignored, and mercifully, Mitch and Jordy were ignored too. Three o'clock came without any red cards in their lockers. And since The Syndicate never hassled them on the weekend, they looked forward to a couple of stress free days. Unfortunately, it was not to be.

***

There was an ongoing Nature Film Series at church on Friday evenings, and Mitch attended – well -- religiously. The church had a video projection system with a blu-ray player and a very good sound system, and it was almost as good as a movie theater. They were running a series from the BBC called *Planet Earth* which presented some of the most spectacular images of wildlife that Mitch had ever seen. So, for two hours, Mitch was transported to distant corners of the planet, places he would probably never see in person, and was enthralled at the diversity of nature and the glories of God and His creations. Mitch felt safe at church, even when he went there alone – which was the rule, rather than the exception. Aunt Sally's idea of church was watching Reverend Taggart on TV. Jordy belonged to a different church, and usually only went with his mom, and besides, he wasn't all that interested in nature shows. So Mitch went by himself, and the only thing that would have made it perfect was if Bagel could have been with him. But even if dogs had been allowed in church, Bagel was not so keen on animal shows: he always freaked out when he heard monkeys chattering or big cats growling on TV.

***

It was about 9:30 when Mitch bicycled up to his walkway. For a change, Aunt Sally had the local news on, and Mitch could hear it outside. "Authorities have dropped the charges against Restaurateur Tommy Rayburn for lack of evidence. Rayburn allegedly ran a prostitution ring involving area high school girls and waitresses at his establishment..."

As Mitch entered, he saw a study in contrasts: obese Aunt Sally, munching Fritos on her La-Z-Boy, while the TV showed this Tommy Rayburn guy in his strip club called "Jugs," surrounded by some very pretty – and scantily clad – young girls.

"More smut on the news," muttered Aunt Sally, switching the channel. "Disgusting filth."

"Hi, Aunt Sally. Hey, Bagel! C'mere boy!"

But Bagel didn't come.

"Bagel? Where are you, Bagel?" Mitch looked all around. "Aunt Sally, where's Bagel? Did you let him out?"

"No, I thought he was with you."

"I told you I went to church. They don't allow dogs at church."

"Well, he wasn't here when I got home."

"You mean, you went out?"

"Just to the market. Oh, some girl called."

"A girl? What girl? Who? Was it Amy?"

"I don't know. Said she'd call back."

A *girl* called him? Girls *never* called him. But that was the least of his concerns right now. "Bagel? Here, Bagel!"

Mitch entered his bedroom and noticed that the window was open. Weird. He didn't recall leaving it open. He stuck his head out. "Bagel! Come home!" God forbid that Bagel had gone out looking for him. It happened once a couple of years ago, and

Mitch had been terrified for hours until the pup found his way back home. Just thinking about it made him wheeze. He gasped, took a hit from his inhaler, and caught his breath.

The phone rang. Mitch answered it, taking it as far from Aunt Sally as he could. "Hello?"

Yes, it *was* a girl, and it was the very last girl Mitch would have expected.

"Wheezer, this is Kellie."

Mitch scowled. "What do *you* want? Uh, Miss Kellie?"

"Don't hang up, it's serious. I know you've got no reason to believe me, but Doug's amped up and gone crazy. He and Winter took your dog."

"What? They took Bagel? Oh my God. Oh my God! Is he all right?"

"Yeah, but I'm really scared of what they're gonna do. I know I've never been nice to you, but even I don't want to see a little dog get hurt."

"Where is he? I'll call the cops!"

"No, no, no. If the cops show up, who knows what'll happen. But I'll swing by and take you to him so you can rescue him."

"Okay, great. Thank you so much, Kellie. I love Bagel, I don't what I'd do if anything happened to him. Do you know where I live?"

"Yes. I've got your address. I'll be there soon." She ended the call.

Mitch sighed. So much for a peaceful weekend. This was as low as it got, and even as Mitch feared for Bagel, he seethed with hate for Doug Niles. He needed three shots from his inhaler to catch his breath.

“I'm going out to find Bagel,” he announced to Aunt Sally, and he was out the door before she could respond.

Mitch walked up the gravel road that was the only route to their mobile home. No reason to risk his Aunt seeing him get into a car with a girl, because he'd never hear the end of *that*.

***

Kellie drove a white Mustang and Mitch waved her down. Mitch started to get in the front.

“No,” she said. “Get in back, lie on the floor. I can’t let anybody see you with me.”

“Okay, sure.”

“Just lie on the floor. It'll take us about 20 minutes to get there.”

“Where?”

“A cabin in the woods Doug uses for parties and stuff. It's his Dad's.”

Mitch had heard about “The Cabin,” but he hadn't heard anything more than what Kellie just told him. All sorts of scenarios and thoughts ran through his mind during the drive. One thought in particular struck him, because it was something that Pastor Phelps had said. “There's good in everyone.” Mitch had never thought there was any good in Kellie, but she was certainly proving him wrong tonight. At the same time, Mitch worried what would happen if he encountered Niles or Winter. Simply put, Mitchell Simon was terrified.

Chapter 8

Mitch had absolutely no idea where they were. The rural highway was dark, and finally Kellie turned off onto an unpaved road. “Almost there,” she said.

Mitch cautiously lifted his head. The Mustang pulled up a gravel driveway past a picket fence and parked in back of the dimly lit "cabin," which was actually a decent sized vacation house. Mitch could see that there were a number of cars parked off to the side, and he could hear pounding rap music from inside. Kellie got out with a grocery bag of food, and called out loudly.

“It's me, Doug! I got the stuff!” Then she whispered to Mitch. “The back door's unlocked. I'll go around the front and keep 'em occupied. The dog's in a kennel in the dining room, so you'll have to creep in there very quietly. Once you get him, keep him quiet and run like hell. You'll have to find your own way home – hitchhike, walk, I don't care, it's your problem, not mine. This is as much as I'm doing.”

“Okay. Thanks again, Kellie.”

“Oh, and one more thing: this never happened, right?

“Right.”

She went around to the front door, while Mitch quietly crept along another picket fence to the back. He took a deep breath and then pulled open the screen door. Then he turned the handle on the back door. Sure enough, it opened. Mitch entered. His heart was pounding, but not quite as hard or as loud as the music. Which was a good thing – the music would cover any noise he might make.

Mitch tiptoed across the kitchen. Through a doorway, he saw a Travel Kennel in the dimly lit dining room, and Bagel was sleeping peacefully inside. Thank God! Mitch took a deep breath -- then wheezed: the air smelled of tobacco and dope. He quickly used his inhaler to stabilize his breathing. He concentrated, thinking, *quiet, Bagel, please be quiet...*

Mitch moved through the doorway, taking one step, then another, and another...

Bagel remained asleep.

Almost there now, Mitch was almost to the kennel. He bent down, closer...

Suddenly, a door slammed and lights came on! Bagel awoke with a yelp.

"Surprise, sucker!" laughed Kellie.

Mitch was shocked to find himself surrounded by some 30 kids, including Niles, Winter and Deuce. Cam aimed his HD-Cam at him – he was recording everything. It was all a set-up, and he fell for it, hook line and sinker. Pastor Phelps was completely wrong: there was no good in Kellie.

Niles laughed loudly. "Look who's been waiting for you, Wheezer!"

They shoved Mitch into the adjoining living room where he saw Jordy gagged and bound to a chair, clad only in his underwear. He was covered with food remnants from being pelted. Jordy looked at Mitch with a pained expression.

"We told him if he didn't come and play striptease target practice, we'd break both your arms," explained Niles as he took a pull on a flask of Jim Beam. "What a sap! You fags really love each other, don't ya? Well, tonight we're gonna see how much."

Mitch said nothing. He looked around at the Hard Corps doing booze, bongs and blunts. A hookah was getting a lot of attention, and powder was being snorted as well. Everybody was on something, but Mitch was too ignorant to identify any of the substances. He also noticed a tray full of cellphones under a sign, "What happens in The Cabin stays in The Cabin." It was especially critical for Niles to have compete control over everything that happened on these premises – his father had made that clear as a condition for using it, and Frank Niles wasn't about to risk having photos and videos of illegal activities on his property finding their way to the police or the press. Only Cam was allowed to record here.

"Kill the tunes – it's showtime!" proclaimed Niles.

Someone turned off the music.

Niles swaggered around Mitch. "Now, Wheezer: I hate dogs,

so I don't give a fuck whether your stupid mutt lives or dies. But if you do, you're gonna do every fucking thing we say."

"Okay," agreed Mitch, "just please don't hurt him!"

Winter laughed. "This is gonna be awesome!"

Deuce pulled out a pair of cigarettes and lit them off the flames in the fireplace.

Niles continued. "Now the other day, you said you were faggots. But some of the gang here didn't believe it. Since we don't want anyone to think you're liars, we decided for tonight's entertainment, we'd have you do each other."

Mitch gasped. "Wait – you don't mean you want us to --?"

Kellie snickered malevolently. "Suck, suck, suck!"

Winter removed Jordy's gag.

"You're sick, Niles! You're sick!" he said.

"Hey, you're the one who said he was a fag! *That's* sick! Now this sorta thing is always more fun with a time limit. But nobody's gonna know for sure what the time limit is." With that, Niles stepped over to a rope with a hangman's noose that dangled from a rafter and pulled a tall bar stool under it. This made it a crude gallows. "And we don't know because no one knows how long the fucking mongrel can hang with his neck in this noose before he dies!"

Kellie took Bagel out of the kennel and brought him over to the "gallows." The beagle sat on the bar stool as Kellie put the noose around his neck, with no idea what was about to happen.

Mitch was horrified. “Geez, you guys! That's my dog! I'll do whatever you want, but please don't hurt my dog!”

Niles's eyes flashed with menace, and he slapped Mitch hard across his face. “Hey, I fuckin' *hate* dogs, bitch! And don't you *ever* tell me what to do, understand?”

Jordy was in just as much disbelief as Mitch. “C'mon, somebody here, please stop this! You can't let 'em kill his dog!”

But his plea fell on deaf ears.

Now Winter spoke up. “Hey, whether the mutt lives or dies is up to you two. I mean, we don't wanna hurt nobody. We just want you guys to do what fags do all the time...and it doesn't hurt them. Hell, they enjoy it. I think you will too. I know *we* will!”

Niles grabbed Mitch by the collar. “Wheezer sucks first. On your knees, bitch.”

Mitch's eyes filled with tears. “Don't hurt Bagel, please don't hurt Bagel. I'll do it, just don't --”

Niles slapped him again. “Shut up, cry baby, and do what we tell you!”

Mitch dropped to his knees.

“Bring Shrimpboat over,” barked Niles.

Deuce and Winter untied Jordy's bonds, pulled him off the chair, stood him in front of Mitch and yanked down his briefs. They held his arms tightly so he couldn't escape.

The Hard Corps responded with whoops and hollers while Cam captured everything with his HD-Cam.

Mitch closed his eyes. This was not exactly a pleasant view. Niles yanked his hair. "Open your eyes, bitch! This is something a girl can do, so there's no reason why you can't do it too!"

Mitch opened his eyes and looked at Jordy's penis in his face.

Niles grinned sadistically. "When I kick the bar stool out from under your pooch, you better start suckin', bitch. Your dog's life is in your hands. Or should I say, your mouth!" Niles stepped over toward the bar stool. "On your mark! Get set! *Suck!"*

He kicked the stool out from under Bagel. The helpless animal gasped as his neck was pulled. He was suspended in air, flailing and whimpering.

Mitch was crying. His mind was in a hellish haze. He didn't know what to do.

The crowd started chanting, "Suck, suck, suck..."

Jordy closed his eyes. He couldn't look at anything – he wanted to shut all of his senses down.

Mitch's face was contorted. Could he do this? He looked over at Bagel: his poor dog flailed helplessly as he gasped for air.

Everything seemed to be moving in slow motion.

The chanting got louder: "Suck! Suck! Suck! Suck!"

Mitch's head and heart were pounding.

Sweat poured from his face.

Cam's lens was right in Mitch's face, and then in Jordy's crotch.

Niles cackled with glee, and Kellie, Winter and Deuce shared his sick satisfaction.

"Suck! Suck! Suck! Suck!"

Suddenly, there was a loud BANG that sounded like a gunshot. But it wasn't: the front door had been kicked open. Heads turned and the chanting stopped.

There stood *James Batt.* But his demeanor was totally different than that of the wimpy, sissy boy of a few days ago. In jeans and an open white windbreaker, he was determined, intense and resolute. He stood up straight, and his voice was strong and direct. "Let the dog go."

Everyone stared, but no one made a move.

Jordy and Mitch now focused on Batt.

Niles responded, "I see nothing, I hear nothing!"

Batt stepped toward him. "*Let the dog go. Asshole.*"

Niles glared at him. "Make me."

There was a moment of tension and dead quiet as the two faced each other. But the quiet was interrupted when Bagel whimpered again.

Batt suddenly reached inside of his jacket and pulled out a knife with a wide, six-inch blade. It glinted in the light.

Niles laughed. "What? You're gonna kill me?"

No. Batt balanced the blade, then *threw* it: it whizzed through the air, past Niles, and *severed the hangman's rope*, imbedding in the wall behind it! It was a knife throw that would have made any circus performer proud.

Bagel dropped to the floor with a yelp.

Mitch scrambled over to him, pulled the noose off of his neck and cuddled him. The dog was fine, thank goodness.

With the distraction, Winter and Deuce had released Jordy, so Jordy pulled up his underwear. Batt called to them. “Mitch, Jordy, we're outta here!”

“Like hell!” screamed Niles. “Nobody leaves unless I say so! And I say, *no!*”

Batt walked up to Niles defiantly and got in his face. “Well, I say, *fuck you.*”

Enraged, Niles grabbed Batt and threw him against the wall. “No, fuck *you*, you sick son of a bitch! So you like pain, do ya?” Niles rammed his head into Batt's chin. “Have some more!” He kneed Batt in the groin. Batt gasped in pain.

The guests enjoyed this and egged Niles on with the old football cheer, “hit him again, hit him again, harder, harder!”

Mitch and Jordy were appalled. They didn't know what to do. Again, the action seemed to be in slow motion. They wanted to do *something,* but they also didn't want to get beaten up. It was one huge, gigantic nightmare.

Not that they could have done anything if they'd tried, because it was then that Niles spied Batt's knife lodged in the wall next to him. He yanked it out.

“And I'll bet you'll really like *this!*” he shouted as he mercilessly stabbed Batt in the stomach.

Batt's eyes opened wide in pain.

Jordy and Mitch were horrified.

Cam, still recording everything, was shocked too.

But no one else was shocked: on the contrary, there were whoops, hollers and cheers. The booze, dope and ecstasy had made everyone's bad judgment even worse.

"Oh, kew-ell!!" shouted Winter as Niles stabbed Batt again. Blood oozed out of Batt's shirt and onto his windbreaker. Batt slumped onto a low table, face up, bleeding.

Niles took a few breaths, then looked down at Batt – not sure if he was still alive -- then looked at the bloody knife, and knew what he had to do. He grabbed Winter and shoved the knife into his hand. "Winter! Do him!"

Winter laughed. "Oh, yeah!" He impaled Batt with a vicious thrust. "That's for wanting to suck my big perfect dick, you sicko!"

There were more whoops and hollers from the guests.

Niles called to Deuce. "Deuce, your turn! Stab the freak!"

Deuce took the knife, posed theatrically for the camera, then stabbed Batt with a victory yell.

There were more cheers from the group. Jordy and Mitch were horrified. This was depravity – complete, total, utter depravity -- and they felt every blow.

Kellie came forward and took the knife from Deuce. "My turn. I hate wimpy fags!" She gave Batt a particularly vicious thrust in the groin.

Niles looked at the rest of the group. Most of them were acting like this was great sport. “Everybody takes a turn!” he proclaimed. “Because if we *all* do him, nobody'll know for sure who *really* did him, right? So nobody'll be responsible! Now, everybody line up and take a stab at him!” Some of them hesitated. “*Everybody!* Rick! Big-E! Janet! Vomit! You too, Lexi!”

Niles and Winter made everyone get into a line. Deuce put the music back on, figuring the driving beat would be “music to stab to.”

“C'mon, you wusses,” taunted Kellie, as she too pulled kids into the line. “It's just like in Julius Caesar! So pretend it's English homework!”

“Yeah!” laughed Winter. “Who'd ever thought we'd learn somethin' from *that* shit!”

Eagerly or reluctantly, each of the Hard Corps did as they were ordered.

Mitch and Jordy turned away, sick to their stomachs, tears in their eyes. It was, for all intents and purposes, a ritual killing. Mitch held Bagel closer and started crying.

One after another, the rest of the kids stabbed Batt while Cam recorded every thrust.

It took less than three minutes, after which Niles killed the music again. “Now everybody, listen up! If anybody talks, tweets, posts, or texts, you're gonna convict yourself, 'cause it's all been recorded! If one of us goes down, we *all* go down! And I'm not going down, because if I do, I'll give 'em the video and drag you *all* down – every single one of ya – with me. We're now all in this together. We're partners!"

There was a moment of silence as he let that thought seep into the clouded brains of his sycophants. Then he gestured at Batt's lifeless form. "Now this fucking freak was *nobody!* He was a sicko pervert, and the world's gonna be a better place without him! We don't know him, we don't know anything about him. And he was never here tonight. You got that? He was *never here*. As far as we're all concerned, he never even existed." Niles noticed Cam aiming his lens at him. "Yo, Cam, I didn't see *you* do him."

"Well, no – I was recording it all."

"Then do it. *Now.*"

Cam hesitated. "But, Doug, I – "

"I said *now*, asshole! If we can do it, you can do it."

Deuce grabbed Cam's camera. "Gimme that. I'll record."

Cam had no choice. He hated himself for doing it, and he hated Doug for making him do it, but he reluctantly picked up the knife and inflicted a rather pathetic wound into Batt's leg.

"Put some feeling into it, geek!" ordered Niles.

Cam took a deep breath, summoned his resolve, then stabbed Batt in a bloody area that was already full of punctures. He left the knife in the body.

“Is that everybody?” asked Niles.

“The stool samples,” said Kellie. “We gotta do something about the stools.”

The Syndicate turned their attention to Jordy and Mitch. The boys were scared and sickened. Niles moved in close to them and spoke quietly. “It's like this, motherfuckers: if you talk? You die. Just like Batt-man. Remember, it'd be your word against 30 of us, and my old man's a lawyer with heavy connections. *Don't go there*. And here's another incentive: you keep quiet, you get a pass. You ignore us, we ignore you. Got it?”

The boys gulped and nodded.

Cam was particularly on edge. “Yo, Doug, we gotta clean this place up and clean ourselves up and dump this body and get the fuck outta here!”

Niles nodded, then turned to the large group. “Everybody *out!* Get drunk, get high, forget everything! This *never happened!* Now, *go!*”

No one had to be told twice.

Chapter 9

Less than seven minutes later, Mitch and Jordy were walking toward town along the rural road that led to The Cabin's driveway. Jordy was now fully clothed, and Mitch carried Bagel. They'd seen the cars of the other kids going that way, and even though they weren't exactly sure where they were or how long it would take them to get home, there was enough moonlight to see, and they knew they'd encounter road signs before too long.

To say that they were devastated would be an understatement. They were both physically and emotionally numb. They didn't know if they were hot or cold or tired or hungry or anything else. They just walked and talked and wondered what they should do.

"Shit, man," said Jordy, "they might kill us anyway. I didn't think they were capable of it, but they are."

"Then we should tell, right?"

"I dunno. They're gonna dump the body, get rid of the evidence. Like Niles said, it could end up being our word against theirs, so us telling might make it worse. And it'd get my mom involved, and that probably doesn't have a happy ending."

"Maybe we should, like, run away or something."

"To where?"

Mitch shrugged and sighed.

“And you know what else?” Jordy added. “I didn't even pay attention to the address on the mailbox. How would we report *that* to the cops?”

“You wanna go back and get it?”

“Hell, no! I never wanna see that place ever again!”

They walked in silence for another minute or so.

“I'm thinking we just bide our time,” said Jordy. “Wait for one of 'em to mess up. Somebody'll talk or text or tweet. 30 kids can't all keep a secret.”

Mitch choked back a tear. “He died to save Bagel, Jordy. And he's not even gonna have a funeral. I'm gonna pray for him. I'm gonna pray for him every day for the rest of my life.”

“Well, you go ahead and pray. Me, I’d say this proves God doesn’t really give a rat's ass about any of this. Bastards. I hope they all suffer for this. I want ‘em *all* to pay.”

“Amen,” said Mitch.

***

Back at The Cabin, Niles and his posse were furiously cleaning blood off the floor and furniture. They had moved Batt's body outside, to deal with later. The fire in the fireplace still burned, and Deuce lit up another pair of cigarettes.

“How the fuck was he able to throw a knife like that?”

wondered Deuce. "That's what I'd like to know."

"How'd the son of a bitch get here?" asked Niles. "How'd he even know where we were?"

"Maybe he followed one of the stools," offered Winter.

"No way," said Cam. "He said he didn't have a car."

Deuce shrugged. "Maybe he lied."

"Hey, Cam," said Niles, "gimme your camera."

Cam handed it to him. Niles popped the SD card out of it.

"What are you gonna do with that?" asked Cam.

Niles tossed the card in the fireplace. In moments it was enveloped in flames and melted. "Like I said: this *never happened.*"

***

Once the place was clean enough, they tackled the big job: the disposing of the body. Lit by moonlight and a large flashlight held by Kellie, the four guys carried Batt's corpse through the woods to the edge of a deep gully several hundred yards away. That's where Niles had decided they would dump it. It was all private property belonging to Frank Niles, so it wasn't like anyone would happen to wander through. And the gully was deep enough that there was no chance of anyone spotting it even if they did. They got into position to throw the corpse. Winter and Deuce had the legs, and Niles and Cam had the arms. They swung it as Niles counted.

"One – two -- three!"

They released it, and it rolled down the gully, into some brush and disappeared from sight. Kellie shined the flashlight down there, and even knowing where to look, they couldn't see it.

"Between the coyotes and the rats and the birds, I figure in a few weeks, there won't be anything recognizable," said Niles.

"Oh, shit" said Cam.

"What?"

"The knife! We left the knife in him! Sure, the body'll decompose and get eaten, but not the knife. Somebody finds that, it'll have our fingerprints on it!"

"There's over 30 different people's prints on it," said Deuce. "No way will they identify anything."

"I dunno," said Cam. "I've seen 'em do some pretty amazing shit on NCIS."

"I ain't worried," said Winter. "But if you are, go down there and get it."

"Yeah, Cam. Go get it. I'll hold the light for you," offered Kellie.

Cam sighed. "No, I guess you guys are right. Besides, after it rains a few times, they won't be able find anything."

"I dunno, Cam," said Deuce. "There was an episode where they got prints off a rusty knife five years after a murder."

Cam looked at him, concerned. "Really?"

"Swear to God," said Deuce. And then he slapped him and

chortled. "Gotcha!"

They all laughed. Except Cam.

***

Needless to say, Jordy and Mitch did not have a pleasant rest-of-the-night. Their walk back took over three hours. Luckily, no cops spotted them or they might have been harassed about curfew violation. It was around two a.m. when they each finally got home.

Mitch's Aunt Sally had fallen asleep in front of the TV, as usual, and Mitch's bedroom door was still closed so he knew she wouldn't ask him about last night. This was one of those times when he was glad she took so little interest in him. He gave Bagel some extra treats and they got into bed. Bagel was just fine, and far less traumatized than he was. After about 15 minutes, Mitch dozed off into an uneasy sleep.

***

Jordy had gotten home to find his Mom's door closed and his sister's door closed. His door was also closed because he usually kept it that way. So he too figured that no one had checked on his whereabouts before they went to sleep. But if he was asked, he'd just say he was hanging out with Mitch, and that would be the end of it.

***

They'd decided to meet at the Route 12 Junkyard. It was one of those places that moms had forever told their sons to stay away from because those old cars were dangerous, so that made it a magnet for boys. It had always been a great place to scavenge for interesting pieces of junk, but today they weren't scavenging. Today they were throwing rocks at wrecked cars, rusty washing machines and rotting refrigerators, imagining they were hitting Niles and the Syndicate. Bagel gnawed happily on the bone Mitch had gotten from Raul at the diner.

"It's so weird," said Mitch. "We prayed they'd leave us alone, and now they *are* gonna leave us alone. Except it's almost worse than if they didn't."

"Yeah. Hey – remember when we asked J.B. if he thought God answered prayers, and he said sometimes, but sometimes the devil does? Maybe that's what's happened. Maybe the devil answered our prayers."

"But we weren't praying to the devil."

"I know. But maybe something happened with all that lightning that night to, y'know, like, scramble the signals or something."

"You really think lightning could interfere with prayers and send 'em to the wrong place?" Mitch asked.

"I dunno, I guess it sounds kinda stupid. But if you're gonna believe in the devil, I guess you can believe that lightning could mess up your prayers."

"So you believe in the devil now, Jordy?"

"I dunno. I dunno what to believe any more. But with this kinda evil, maybe there really *is* a devil. Or Satan. Or the Prince of Darkness. Whatever."

"I hope so. 'Cause that would explain a whole lot."

"So, Mitch -- you're always going to church. Does your minister ever talk about the devil? Or hell?"

Mitch pinged a rock off of hubcap. "Pastor Phelps? Not really, just sorta symbolically. But this guy my Aunt watches on TV talks about it all the time. *He* believes in the devil. And hell. But I don't like him much."

"You ever ask Pastor Phelps if *he* believes in the devil? Or hell?"

"No. But if he did, I think he'd have mentioned it."

"So how come you go to a church where you believe in different stuff from the Pastor?"

Mitch shrugged. "My grandma went to that church and she always took me there. She loved Pastor Phelps, and when she died, he did her funeral, and he was super nice to me. So when I go to services, I feel sorta connected to her. It's like he's family. And I always feel safe when I go there."

Jordy nodded. It made sense.

"Jordy," said Mitch, "why don't you come with me tomorrow? I mean, like, if we ever really needed to pray, this would be that time. And you don't have to wear a tie."

Jordy considered it and nodded. "Okay. Yeah. It couldn't hurt."

***

The Westover Community Church was simple, modest and tasteful in both its building and décor, and aptly reflected Pastor Phelps. Pastor Phelps, about 60, came across as a thoughtful man; he was certainly not one to engage in anything resembling gimmickry to increase attendance or membership. He preferred a more traditional approach, and his congregation was comfortable with that. The Sunday morning service was about half full, which was also traditional.

Mitch always sat in the same place, in the 8th pew, on the left side. Not only was 8 his lucky number, but this was where he used to sit with his grandma, so he couldn't imagine sitting anywhere else. This morning, he was especially happy to have Jordy with him. It was the first time in about two years that he'd not been alone in church on Sunday, because Aunt Sally rarely attended.

The sermon was about forgiveness, which was not a topic with much appeal for Mitch and Jordy today. Still, they listened, even with their doubts.

"For the Lord will forgive even the worst sinner who is repentant in his heart. And he -- or she -- who is so truly repentant and has sought forgiveness from God and from man, then that person shall be redeemed and will be ensured a place in Heaven to share in the glories of God and life everlasting. Amen. Let us pray."

The congregation dropped their heads in prayer.

Mitch whispered his prayer. "God, please bless the soul of James Batt and reward him for saving my dog. May he rest in peace and find some happiness, because he sure didn't get any around here. Amen."

Jordy looked over at Mitch and smiled. Then he bowed his head. "God," said Jordy. "What he said -- times a million trillion. Amen."

Chapter 10

The sunshine beaming down on Woodrow Wilson High School belied the mood which permeated the Junior Class on that Monday morning. Not everyone was aware of it, but Amy certainly was. Certain students were quieter and more restrained than usual, and that brought everyone else down. Amy turned to her friend Katie. "Did something happen over the weekend? It's like somebody died, or something."

"I know, right?" said Katie. "It's...weird."

***

As usual, Mr. Tidrow began his 2nd Period Algebra Class by taking attendance. "Adams?"

"Here."

"Atkins?"

"Here."

"Baden?"

"Here."

"Batt?"

There was no response.

"James Batt? Anybody know if the new kid is in school today?"

No one responded. Jordy and Mitch exchanged an uneasy look. Winter looked over at them and gave them the eye. They saw it, and Winter saw that they were going to be good, quiet little soldiers.

Mr. Tidrow shrugged and marked him absent. "Brimley?"

"Here."

"Carswell?"

"Here."

Roll call continued. There were no other absences.

***

Jordy and Mitch sat quietly in the lunchroom, gnawing on their sandwiches. Mitch washed a bite of his turkey down with a swallow of milk. "Don't you think it's weird they haven't made an announcement or anything? I mean, like, wouldn't his mom have reported him missing?"

"Maybe she doesn't know," said Jordy. "Maybe she's out of town. We don't even know if he lived with his parents. We really didn't know anything about him."

Now Amy came over and sat right down, intense and direct. "So. Gentlemen. There's a rumor that something happened to J.B. Friday night. Something really, really bad. So what's up?"

Jordy and Mitch traded a knowing look.

Jordy shrugged. “We don't know. We haven't seen him.”

“Duh!” she said. “No one else has either. I thought maybe you guys knew something. Like, did you talk to him over the weekend?”

“No,” answered Mitch. “We don’t have his phone number.”

“He's your friend! Aren't you at all concerned?”

“Maybe he's sick, Amy. Just 'cause he's absent one day is no big deal.”

“What about the rumors?”

“We don't know about any rumors,” said Mitch. “We're not exactly 'connected.'”

“I heard you were there,” she said.

“Where?” asked Jordy.

“Wherever it happened!”

“Where *what* happened?”

“I don't know, but I'm gonna find out.” She walked off in a frustrated huff.

Jordy looked at Mitch. “I told you somebody would talk. Now it's just a matter of time.”

“You think we could get in trouble for not reporting it?”

But before Jordy could answer, there was a loud **bang** that sounded like – well, it sounded just like that loud bang on Friday night.

Every head turned in direction of the sound. And quite a

number of those faces reacted with total astonishment because, standing there in the entryway, perfectly fine, was *James Batt.* At his feet, next to those distinctive dirty orange tennis shoes, was a thick textbook. "Sorry to startle everyone. I dropped my history book." He bent down to pick it up.

Mitch and Jordy were stunned.

Niles, the Syndicate, and the Hard Corps kids were equally stunned.

Batt stood up and looked around at everyone. He stood taller, his hair was clean and combed, and the black T-shirt and jeans he wore fit him better. If he had looked like this last week, it was doubtful he would have been considered a target.

He could see that everyone was staring at him, but he behaved as if nothing had ever happened. The truth was, his manner was more upbeat than anyone had ever seen. He calmly went to Jordy and Mitch and smiled. "Hey, guys. Hey, Mitch, how's your dog? Everything okay with him?"

Jordy's jaw dropped. Mitch's breath got short, and he wheezed, so he took a hit from his inhaler, and in a few moments caught his breath.

"F-f-fine, J.B. He's fine."

"That's good. I love dogs. Always have. They're good friends. Better than people."

Jordy gulped. "So...what's up with you, J.B.?"

Batt grinned. "I overslept."

Jordy shook his head and lowered his voice. “C'mon, man, what the hell is really going on here?”

Batt's response was far less jovial. “Ask me no questions, I'll tell you no lies. And trust me, sometimes curiosity can be dangerous.” Batt was aware of the number of people staring at him. “They're all looking at us, and since I officially "don't exist," you guys could get in deep shit for talking to me. Although, confidentially? I don't think that's gonna last much longer. Later.”

Batt walked away, leaving the two boys totally dumbfounded.

“He *died*, right?” said Mitch. “I mean, they killed him! We saw it! He was *dead*!”

Jordy rubbed his chin. “Well, he's sure not dead now.”

***

Batt strode confidently over to Niles's table. He glared at them, one by one, and they looked back at him briefly, uncomfortably, and then tried not to meet his gaze. Batt looked straight at Niles. “So. Doug. You got something to say to me?”

Batt focused on Niles with an intense, piercing, probing stare. Niles didn't like those eyes. Did he imagine it or did they seem to momentarily change color? He looked away and shook his head.

Batt now looked at Winter. “What about you, Mr. Guy-With-The-Perfect-Dick?”

Winter ignored him. He had nothing to say.

Batt looked at Deuce. "How about you, Double Cancer-Man?"

Deuce looked away.

"Or you, Geek Camera Boy?"

Cam dropped his head.

Batt turned his unnerving stare on Kellie, then put on a southern accent.

"Or you, *Miss* Kellie, mistress of the plantation?"

She met his stare with her own disdainful version, but even she looked away after a few moments.

They all tried to ignore Batt, but Batt wasn't about to be ignored. He leaned in next to Niles and spoke loudly. "Well, I've got something to say to *you*, Doug..."

Niles looked at him with uncertainty. Everyone in the vicinity turned to watch, including Mr. Cutler.

Batt lowered his voice. "You shouldn't eat this crap." And with a sudden swipe of his arm, Batt sent Niles's tray of food onto the floor. CRASH!

Mr. Cutler took a step toward them and cleared his throat loudly. "Do we have a problem over there, gentlemen?"

Batt replied, "Gee, sir, I don't know, but I can find out for you, sir." He then turned to Niles and did his best Mr. Cutler imitation, even clearing his throat first. "Do we have a problem, Mr. Niles?"

Niles hesitated, then called back to Cutler. "No, Mr. Cutler. No problem, sir."

Cutler was not amused. “Mr. Batt! My office. In exactly ten minutes.”

“Yes, sir.” Batt turned back to Niles and The Syndicate. “Catch you guys later.”

He walked away, leaving a very uneasy group of assholes. Nobody wanted to make the first comment, but Niles could see they were all waiting for him to say something.

“I don't know, okay?” barked Niles. “I don't fuckin' know! It doesn't make sense! It doesn't make any fuckin' sense!”

They were all quiet for several moments.

“Well, I know one thing,” said Cam with a tone of relief. “At least we're not guilty of murder.”

***

Batt took a seat in Mr. Cutler's office. Various diplomas and awards hung on the walls, and a few photos sat on the shelves, all trying to give the impression that the occupant was qualified and dedicated. The Counselor looked up from a file. “We haven't received a transcript from your last school, Mr. Batt. I called them, and they said it's because they never got a transcript from the school previous to them.”

“It's sad, isn't it, sir? That so many schools are run by underpaid, overworked incompetent bureaucrats who are just buried in paperwork?”

"I saw what you did in the cafeteria. I won't have trouble here, Mr. Batt."

"Well, sir, I simply expect to be treated the same way you've treated Doug Niles and his friends."

"How do you know you're not being treated the same way?"

Batt gave him *the stare*. Sharp. Intense. Piercing. Drilling right into him. For an instant, Cutler thought those eyes changed colors. Batt calmly answered. "I know. Sir."

Mr. Cutler felt uncomfortable, almost as if he was being threatened. But Batt had said nothing nor done anything that could be defined that way. Cutler cleared his throat. "I'd like to talk to your parents. How can I contact your father?"

"My father. You want to contact my father. Do you mean My Father Who Art In Heaven, or the guy who impregnated my mother? Because the first one is easy to contact, only He's not real good at answering. The other guy, I never met. Don't know if he's alive or dead. And I don't wanna know."

Ouch. Mr. Cutler had stepped in it, although, without a file on this kid, there was no way he could have avoided it. His manner softened. "I'm sorry. What about your mother?"

"She's had a rough life, Mr. Cutler. You talking to her isn't gonna make it any better."

"I still want to set a meeting. The three of us. You'll be included, and everything will be above board."

Batt nodded agreeably. "Fine, sir. Let's do it. But let's do it *after* you have a meeting with Chrissy Anderson and her parents. I know you'll all have a *lot* to talk about."

Cutler's face went white and his jaw dropped.

Batt continued. "Do you still have the Range Rover? With those striped cushions in the back? Oh – no – wait – you had to sell it to pay for the abortion, right?"

Mr. Cutler's voice dropped to a shocked whisper. "*How do you know about that?*"

Batt responded politely. "I did my homework, sir. And from the looks of it, I got an A, didn't I?"

Cutler said nothing and dropped his head in shame.

Batt cleared his throat. "Would you like me to try for some extra credit, sir?"

Cutler sighed in defeat. "Just leave."

So Batt left. He left a very unnerved Mr. Cutler to stew in the juices of his own hypocrisy. Batt was smiling.

***

After Fifth Period, Jordy and Mitch caught up with Batt at his locker. "So, J.B., seriously? What actually happened to you Friday night?" asked Jordy.

Batt smiled wryly. "I got killed."

"C'mon, man, you don't expect us to believe that."

Batt's demeanor darkened. "Listen, I'm trying to look out for you guys, so trust me: you're better off not knowing. Just back off. And remember: actions have consequences."

Batt slammed his locker shut and walked away.

Mitch couldn't believe his sudden change in attitude. "Whoa. Last week he was pretty nice, now he's...I dunno, different..."

Jordy nodded as an idea came to him. "Maybe it's not him..."

Mitch gave him a look that said, *what on earth are you talking about?*

"Maybe he's got, like, a twin brother or something."

"C'mon, man, that's crazy!"

"It'd make sense, wouldn't it? I mean, it's the only explanation that makes any sense."

"Then how come this "brother" hasn't been going to school here too?"

Jordy thought a moment. "Okay, maybe he's not a *twin* brother. Maybe he's, like, an older brother who looks a lot like him."

"Then how did older brother Batt even know what happened? How could he know to ask my about my dog?"

Jordy sighed. Clearly, his theory had some holes in it. "Okay, okay, so maybe I didn't think it through."

Mitch snickered and headed to his Biology Class. "I'd sooner believe he's the walking dead."

"Well, we didn't see him eating any human flesh," Jordy called out.

"We didn't see him eating *anything*."

Jordy pondered the situation with a troubled expression. He had to know more.

***

Shortly after three o'clock, Niles and The Syndicate and some of the Hard Corps were congregating in the west parking lot. Cam spotted him first.

"Heads up, Doug, we got company."

They all looked toward school. Batt-man was heading their way. And no one was remotely happy about it.

Batt walked right up to Niles. "So, Doug: I got this feeling there's something you wanna ask me. Is there?"

Niles glared at him with total disdain. "No."

"I think you're lying. I think there *is* something you wanna ask me, but you're too chicken to, because you don't wanna hear the answer."

Niles turned away.

Batt taunted him. "Buck, buck, buck, buck buck."

That had the desired effect. Niles gave him a withering stare. "All right, yeah, I got a question for ya, Batt-man: how was your weekend?"

Deuce and Winter chortled.

Batt grinned, then addressed them all. "My weekend. Well, I

went to this really fucked up party Friday night where a buncha major assholes thought they could get away with murder. And after that, I slept like the dead."

Kellie had had enough of this posturing. "Let's get outta here."

"Oh, kiddies?" said Batt. "Just a suggestion. Go to the police. Take 'em out to a certain gully in the woods not far from a certain cabin. Tell 'em everything. Confess -- to that, and everything else you've done. Actually, why wait? You can call 'em right now." Batt pulled a flip phone out of his pocket and tossed it to Niles.

Niles caught it, then hurled it to the ground as hard as he could. The phone cracked apart.

"So that would be "no?"" asked Batt. "Well, just remember: actions have consequences."

Niles got right in his face and poked him in the chest. "Listen, shit stain, I dunno what kinda scam you're pulling here, but I'm warning you: *stay away from me*."

"Wow," said Batt. "Really? You really just said that? You want *me* to stay away from you? That's funny, Doug. Because last week when I *tried* to stay away from you, you kept "inviting" me to join you. I thought you wanted me to be your bitch?" He put on his gayest voice and made a limp-wristed gesture. "What's wrong, sweetie, don't you love me anymore?"

Niles grabbed him by the collar and threw him against a car.

"You stay the fuck away from me, faggot, or you'll regret it!"

"I'll "regret it?" What are you gonna do? *Kill me*?" Batt laughed.

Niles growled. "You don't know who you're fucking with, man."

They all walked off and got in their cars. Batt watched them leave. Then he smiled knowingly, picked up his broken phone and squeezed it in his hand.

"No, Douglas Kenneth Niles, you don't know who *you're* fucking with."

Batt opened his hand: the flip phone was perfectly restored.

Chapter 11

The two-story wood framed house at 4377 Glasser Road was in a decaying neighborhood of foreclosures. The yard was overgrown, the house was badly in need of paint, and it appeared to be abandoned. But unlike some of the other houses on the street, there was no “For Sale” or “Foreclosed” sign in front. The boys got off their bikes. They'd never been to this part of town before.

“Really?” asked Mitch. “*Here?* No way he lives here.”

Jordy shrugged. Even though the “4” on the address number was barely visible, it was definitely the 4300 block, so this had to be it. Jordy had gotten the address from the attendance office. He'd stopped in there after school and told them that he'd found Batt's notebook and wanted to return it to him, but he didn't know the address. The office lady checked with Doctor Jones who stuck her head out to see who was asking. When she saw it was Jordy, she nodded.

“C'mon,” said Jordy, heading up the broken walkway to the weather beaten front door. “Let's scope it out.”

Mitch hesitated. “I don't know if this is a good idea. I mean, he told us to back off. He said curiosity could be dangerous.”

“We'll just look in the windows. He won't even know we're here.”

“What are we even looking for?”

“Like, a family photo or something. Anything that could, like, give us a clue about who he is or where he came from.”

“Hey, look!” said Mitch, pointing to mailbox on the doorway. “Mail! Let's see who it's addressed to.”

Indeed, the mailbox had a number of items sticking out. Mitch took them and went through them. Jordy grabbed some as well. But it was all junk, addressed to “Occupant.” “Resident.” “Our friends.” “Homeowner.”

The boys proceeded around the side of the house and looked through the dirty windows. There wasn't much to see – just a few pieces of beat up furniture, but no personal items and no evidence that anyone lived here. Mitch got some windowsill dust in his face and wheezed.

The back yard was covered in tall weeds. Jordy noticed that a glass window pane in the back door was broken. He reached through it to the doorknob and opened the door.

“It's open! Let's check it out!”

“But we're breaking and entering!” said Mitch.

“We're not breaking, we're just entering.”

Jordy entered. Mitch took a deep breath and reluctantly followed him inside.

They were in the kitchen, and from the look of it, no one lived here at all except cockroaches. Jordy flipped a light switch, but nothing happened. Either there was no electricity or no light bulb. Then he opened the refrigerator. It was dark, empty and stank, so that answered that question. He quickly closed it. Mitch ran his finger along a counter: the dust was really thick. "Hasn't been dusted in months," whispered Mitch. "What if J.B.'s a vampire?"

Jordy answered in a whisper. "Vampires don't go out in the day. And besides, they're not real."

Jordy walked into the living room. Mitch followed.

"What if they *are* real and they *do* go out in the day? I mean, he did come back from the dead, right?"

"Well, then --"

There was a *creak*! It sounded like it came from upstairs. "Sssshhh!" whispered Jordy. They listened. They heard it again. Could it be...footsteps?

They exchanged a worried look and listened some more. Thump. Thump. Yes, definitely footsteps. Someone was descending the stairs!

The boys backed up toward a wall so as not to be seen. Their hearts were pounding. Jordy gritted his teeth. Being here suddenly didn't seem like such a good idea.

The footsteps got louder.

Jordy felt the wall behind him and he pushed back against it, trying to make himself as small as possible. Mitch leaned back against a door, but it wasn't completely closed – it shut with a

LOUD THUD!

The footsteps abruptly stopped: *the boys had been heard!*

They froze in terror. Mitch clutched his chest – he was on the verge of an asthma attack. He struggled to keep himself under control.

Jordy gestured that they should make their way around the back of the stairway. They moved in that direction, and –

– they heard more footsteps – quiet footsteps – so --

-- they turned the corner behind the staircase, and --

"YAAAAAA!!!!"

They were face to face with Amy Danforth who was screaming as well!

And then things got quiet as they all took a few moments to catch their breaths.

"Jeez, Amy," said Jordy, "you almost gave me a heart attack!"

"You almost gave *me* one!"

Mitch was wheezing, having an intense asthma attack.

"Mitch! Mitch! You all right?" Jordy hit him in the chest.

Mitch's eyes were closed as he gasped for air. Jordy reached into his friend's pants pocket, and found his inhaler. He forced it into Mitch's hand. Mitch felt it, gripped it, and gave himself a hit. And another. His gasping stopped. He caught his breath.

"Are you okay, Mitch?" asked Amy, concerned. She looked to Jordy. "Is he okay?"

Mitch nodded. "I'm okay. I'm fine. But let's not do *that*

again."

"Agreed," said Amy. "So who died and made you guys CSI?"

"Same one who made you 'Buffy,'" replied Jordy.

She chuckled. So did he.

"Can we *please* get out of here?" asked Mitch.

***

She bought them Frosties at Wendy's and she got herself a coffee. She would have preferred Starbucks, but Wendy's was closer, and Mitch wanted a Frosty, so the least she could do was make him happy. And as they sat there enjoying their treats, they told her everything – well, almost everything – that happened Friday night.

"I know it sounds insane," said Jordy as he concluded their account, "but it's true." Jordy had omitted some of the specific details of what Niles had expected them to do to each other, and thankfully, she hadn't pressed them on it. At this point, it was the least important part of what occurred, and Jordy got the feeling that she really wasn't interested.

"I *would* think it was insane except I heard the exact same thing from four other people."

Jordy gave Mitch a knowing look. "I told you somebody would talk."

Amy was more curious than ever. "And the fact that he's got, like, a fake address, no phone number... I mean, who is he? Where'd he come from?

"We dunno," said Mitch.

"You guys are his friends and you didn't even try to find out?"

"Hey, we asked him, but he never wanted to talk about it. We're guys. We respect that. I mean, like, there's things that's happened to us that we'd never talk about, either."

"Like what?" she asked.

"Duh! Hello-oh?" answered Jordy.

"Boys are so weird," she said, shaking her head.

"Girls are so weirder," he replied.

They both giggled.

"Okay, next question. Do you know where they dumped the body?"

The boys shook their heads.

"Only five people would know that," said Mitch.

"Six," corrected Jordy.

Chapter 12

Two flashlight beams sliced through the chilly night fog as Niles and The Syndicate made their way down the gully. They'd hoped to get there in the daylight, but Winter had a therapist appointment that he'd canceled twice before, and he knew his mom would be pissed if he canceled it a third time, and then she'd tell his old man, and he'd *really* be pissed, and Winter absolutely did not want to piss off his old man again. Winter had said they could go without him, but that was a non-starter. They were all in this together and that was how it was going to be. Besides, even the faintest suggestion that Winter might be chicken was enough to ensure his presence. And to make doubly sure that they'd all stick together, they decided to come in one vehicle: Winter's Escalade. It was the biggest, and there was plenty of room in the back for shovels.

They'd all fortified themselves with a few drinks, all except Cam, who had trouble holding his liquor. Kellie carried one flashlight and Cam had the other – these were the lantern size types used for camping. For the first time in who-knew-when, Cam did not have lenses strapped to his arms or equipment weighing down his pants. No one saw any upside to him recording anything, especially not Cam. After all, no recordings meant no evidence.

The Cabin was lit up behind them, but even with all of its lights on, it did not provide any illumination at this distance. The night sounds of crickets, frogs and owls, which would have been benign on a camping trip, were downright creepy and menacing in the fog.

“I still say he scammed us with a trick knife and special effects.” said Winter.

“It didn't seem like a trick knife to me,” said Cam.

“Yeah? What do you know about knives?”

“I know that when they cut into something and blood comes out that they're real.”

“So maybe he had his shirt rigged with fake blood. A buncha plastic bags filled with fake blood, just like in the movies.”

“He wasn't breathing, Winter.”

“How would we know? We were drunk and high and trippin'.”

“*I* wasn't.”

“Quit yappin' and keep lookin'!” ordered Niles. “It's the only way we'll know for sure!”

A section of the overcast sky was briefly illuminated by distant lightning flashes. Thunder rumbled a few moments later.

“Great. Just what we need” muttered Cam.

They moved along further, but slowly, in order to keep their footing on the downhill slope. Kellie and Cam lit the way. Then

Deuce stopped suddenly. “Ssshh! I just heard something!”

Everyone stopped and listened. There was a rustling sound. It wasn't the wind blowing through the trees because there was no wind. It could have been an animal.

They kept listening. After another rumble of thunder, they heard it again.

“I bet it's *him,* said Cam. “I bet he's out here – gonna nail us.”

They all remained perfectly still and listened.

Suddenly, a *cell phone rang*! Everyone jumped!

“It's mine,” said Kellie.

“Turn that sucker off!” Niles told her.

“Wait,” said Cam. “What if it's HIM?”

They all traded nervous looks. Kellie took out her iPhone and checked the display. *Unknown Caller.* It rang again. Finally, she took a deep breath and answered it.

“Hello...?” she said cautiously. Then she sighed relief. “Oh, hey, Uncle Tommy, hi. Yeah, I'm fine. Tomorrow after school? Sure, but can I call you back for the details? I'm with some friends right now.” She listened a moment more. “Okay, cool. Later.” She ended the call and looked at the others. “Sorry -- family stuff. My uncle doesn't text.”

They returned to the search. They played their beams over a section of ground at the bottom of the gully, and then they saw it: *a human leg.* It was sticking out of some brush about 10 yards away. Its foot was toe-down, and on it was a dirty orange shoe with that weird logo. *Batt's shoe*. The rest of the body was hidden.

"Special effects, my ass," said Deuce. "He's there just like we left him."

"Shit!" said Winter, his voice actually breaking with worry. "Then who was in school today?"

After a few moments of uneasy silence, Cam spoke up. "His twin brother! It's the only explanation! He's got a twin who wants revenge on us!"

"That's the dumbest shit I ever heard!" said Niles.

No one said anything for a full fifteen seconds.

"Okay, maybe it's dumb," offered Cam, "but you got any better ideas?"

They all stood staring for a few more moments, and then Kellie said what they were all thinking. "How do we know for sure that's really him down there? I just see a leg with a shoe."

They all looked at each other, knowing that there was only one way to find out. In uneasy silence, they moved closer. Kellie and Cam kept their lights on it, but even at a distance of a few feet, they couldn't see much more through the brush.

"Deuce! Pull him out!" ordered Niles. "Let's see his face."

"*Me?* I'm not touching him!"

"What, are you chicken?"

"No, but maybe you are. Maybe that's why you want me to do it!"

Thunder rumbled again, as if the heavens were weighing in

with an opinion.

Niles knew he had no choice now. “I'll show ya,” he said, full of pumped up bravura. “It's just a fuckin' corpse. Can't hurt ya. I mean, we carried the son of a bitch over here on Friday and nothin' happened.”

Niles took a step forward and reached down toward the ankle. He hesitated briefly, swallowed hard, and then he grabbed it. “It's stiff” he said.

“Okay, tough guy, pull him out,” challenged Deuce.

The others watched anxiously. Kellie and Cam steadied their flashlights with both hands.

Niles gave the ankle a yank.

The body was stuck.

He yanked again.

The body moved.

Everyone held their breath.

Niles yanked harder -- the body slowly revealed itself, dressed in the same bloody white windbreaker and jeans as Friday night. But the body was face down. They still couldn't be absolutely sure until they saw the face.

Niles was uneasy. Again the rumble of thunder added to the tension. Finally Niles took a deep breath and rolled it over and --

Gross out! It *was* Batt and *half of his face was decomposed!*

Everyone gasped and jumped back – it was *way* more disgusting than anyone possibly expected.

They all traded nervous looks as they caught their breaths. Kellie and Cam aimed their beams at the decayed face.

"So who the fuck was in school today?" asked Winter.

Suddenly, accompanied by a flash of lightning, Batt jumped up, waving his arms like a monster! *"Meeeeeeeee!"* he yelled.

All five of them screamed in terror and scattered like rats in every direction. Cam and Kellie dropped their flashlights – on the ground, they lit up only dirt.

Niles was behind a tree. He took a moment to catch his breath, then called out, "You guys all okay?"

All four of them called back from the darkness that they were. From the sound of their voices, Niles knew none of them were together.

"Where'd Batt-man go?" he asked.

"Dunno," said Winter.

"Didn't see him," replied Cam.

"Beats me," added Deuce.

Now light rain began to fall. "Shit," said Niles. "Show me the flashlights."

"I dropped mine," said Kellie. "Sorry."

"Same here," answered Cam.

"Damn." Niles thought for a moment. "Okay, everybody, let's all get back to the cabin!"

"Alone?" asked Cam. "Are you crazy? What if Batt-man's gonna ambush us? Kill us off, one by one, just like Jason! I mean, he could be, like, a zombie or a mutant or something!"

Winter made clucking noises. "You chicken, Cam?"

"Hell, yes! And if you're not, you're an idiot!"

Deuce called out. "Yo, morons, I've got a flashlight app. I'll light my phone, you come to where I am and we can go together."

"Good idea!" Cam told him. "You can be the first target!"

There was a long moment of quiet. Niles looked around in the darkness. "C'mon, Deuce, light up your phone!"

Deuce called back uneasily. "Uh, I think my battery's dead..."

Suddenly, a hand clamped down on Niles's shoulder! Niles screamed, turned – and found himself facing Kellie. He sighed.

"Sorry," she said.

"Jesus, Kellie!"

Cam's voice called out. "What happened?"

"Dougie got scared," she said with a touch of amusement. "By little old me." She pulled out her iPhone and lit up the display. "We're over here, you gutless wussies!"

Winter, Deuce and Cam all made their way over to Niles and Kellie. As a group, they retrieved the dropped flashlights and cautiously made their way back toward The Cabin. The light drizzle didn't slow them, but their own fears did. As they moved along, they checked every direction with concern. Every time they heard an owl hoot or any animal sound, they whirled around to see what it was.

"So, you think he's alive or dead?" whispered Cam.

“How the fuck do I know?” replied Winter.

“Did you see his face?” asked Deuce. “I mean, it was, like, decomposed. Like his flesh was chewed up. Man, this is so fucked up.”

Suddenly they heard another animal sound: *Buck, buck, buck, buck, buck, buck.* It was followed by laughter -- Batt's laughter.

They heard his taunting voice. “Oh, the tough guys! The big shots! So cool! So brave! So macho!”

His voice had seemed to come from above. They looked in its direction and saw Batt standing on the cabin's pitched roof with his feet apart to maintain his balance.

“How the hell did he get up there?” whispered Deuce. “Can he fly, too?”

Cam's beam revealed the answer: at one end of the cabin was a ladder leaning up against the structure.

Kellie aimed her light directly at Batt, and he laughed loudly, despite his decomposed face. “A little Halloween makeup and you all turn into wimps!” He tore off the layer of rubber makeup on that side of his face.

“Special effects,” sighed Winter. “Toldja.”

They all felt pretty stupid, which in turn made them feel angry over being fooled.

“Hey, I got your next posting for *Hard Woody 411*,” yelled Batt. “Syndicate shows they're a bunch of chickenshit candy ass pussies!”

“Get down here and we'll see who's a pussy!” challenged Winter.

“Hey, if you're so tough, let's see you come up here and *make* me come down! C'mon, Winter, show your buds that you got enough guts to take me!”

“Do it, Al!” urged Niles. “You can't let him talk to you like that. Go up and push him off!”

Deuce and Kellie echoed Niles's words. Cam, however, was silent.

“Yeah!” said Winter. “I'll take him down.” He yelled up at Batt. “I'm comin' for ya, Batt-man! Be afraid! Be very afraid.”

“Shakin' in my boots,” Batt laughed back.

They all went toward the ladder. The rain was coming down harder now. Cam quietly sidled up to Winter.

“Al,” he said quietly, “it's wet, the roof is sloped – you don't have to do this.”

Winter reacted with a look of total disdain. “Fuck you, you gutless dick. Just gimme some light.”

Cam stepped back and aimed his light at the aluminum ladder. Winter ascended. The rungs were wet, but the treads were cut deep and they weren't slippery. As Winter climbed higher, Cam moved back to keep more light on him.

The others were on the front side of the house, back far enough to see the whole roof. Kellie gave her flashlight to Deuce. “Here. You handle this. Maybe you can blind that asshole.”

Deuce aimed the light at Batt. He was standing near the center of the roof, holding onto the old TV roof antenna for support.

Winter reached the top of the ladder and climbed onto the pitched roof. The rough surfaces of the shingles gave him a bit of traction, but there was no question that the rain was not an asset. Still, if balancing was tricky for him, then it would also be tricky for Batt.

“First one hits the ground's a wuss,” called Batt.

“That'll be you,” answered Winter. He nearly tripped on the wire from the satellite dish, then realized he could use the dormers to balance himself. In a few steps, he found his footing and advanced methodically toward Batt.

Now they faced each other, each trying to psych the other out. Winter feinted right, then left. Batt backed away, almost slipped, then grabbed the antenna for balance.

Winter grinned, sensing an opening. “You're goin' down *now*, motherfucker!”

Winter charged at Batt and rammed him -- the momentum sent them both backward, with Winter on top of Batt --

“You got him, Al, you got him!” Niles yelled excitedly.

But they *both* fell off the roof, out of the light beams and out of view of Niles and the others --

Then -- a *blood curdling scream!*

But whose?

Shit! They all rushed around to the other side to see what had happened. And one by one they reacted in horror as they saw what the light from the cabin illuminated.

"Oh God! Oh Jesus!" shrieked Cam. He turned away, sickened.

Alan Winter was impaled on the picket fence. He was face down, with one fence post literally piercing all the way through his throat, and another picket sticking all the way through his gut. He was still twitching as his blood spurted out. Portions of the white fence were red with blood.

Deuce and Kellie were equally sickened.

"Shit! Where's Batt-man?" Niles shouted.

Shit indeed. From the way they had gone off the roof, Batt should have been impaled on the fence *under* Winter...*yet there was no sign of him anywhere!*

They looked around. Niles grabbed Cam's flashlight and played it all over the area. Deuce did the same with his. Nothing. No footprints in the wet soil, no blood trail, absolutely nothing. The group traded uneasy reactions.

"No way," said Niles. "He couldn't just vanish."

"What if he went inside?" wondered Deuce.

Whoa. That certainly seemed possible.

"Guys," said Cam with rising concern, "what if he went inside, got a butcher knife from the kitchen and he's waiting for us?"

Shit! That too was possible.

"Well, we gotta find out," said Niles. "So we're goin' in there, and we're all gonna stick together, and we're gonna check every room."

They started toward the back door.

"Stop," said Kellie. "Everybody look at your shoes."

Everyone did. They all had mud on them.

"If our shoes have mud on 'em, so would his. So if there's no footprints, he's not inside. And if there are, at least we can be ready."

Yeah, that made sense. Or at least it did until Cam offered an alternate theory. "What if he took off his shoes?"

"Okay, goddammit, listen," said Niles. "We're all goin' together and we're gonna check every room just like I said. Together. And take your fuckin' shoes off! No point in us trackin' mud all over the place. And if he did leave footprints, we'll be able to see 'em."

And that's what they did. They went in together, and they checked every room, and they found absolutely no indication that Batt had gone inside. Everything was exactly as it was. Wherever Batt was, he wasn't in there.

It had taken 15 minutes, and it was now almost 9 o'clock. They plopped down on the chairs in the den, edgy and tense, with a million contradictory thoughts going through their heads. They sat in silence for awhile.

Finally Kellie spoke. “We've gotta report this,” she said definitively.

They all looked at her, unsure. Cam in particular was a mess. “Oh Jesus,” he wailed, “and then what happens? I mean, shit, when the cops get here and we tell 'em about Batt-man, they're gonna investigate and then, if they find out about Friday night, oh my God --”

WHAP!

Kellie slapped his face. “Shut up, you wimp! As far as we're concerned, Batt-man was never here. *Never. Ever.* This was all an accident. A big, stupid, drunken accident. Now let me tell you what *really* happened tonight and what we're gonna say and what we're gonna do...”

Chapter 13

Niles was on TV, being interviewed by an *Action 6 HD News* reporter, telling what had happened – or rather, his version of what had happened. The story was titled “Teenage Tragedy,” and it carried the words, “recorded earlier.”

“So Al went up on the roof to adjust the satellite dish. He'd been drinking -- we all were -- and it was raining, so it musta been slippery up there. About a minute later, we heard him scream.”

The story continued with a Female Reporter at the same scene, in daylight, with the word “live.” She stood near the bloody fence. “Police concur that Alan Winter's death was a tragic, alcohol related accident.”

A Police Captain offered his insight. “Unfortunately, kids do stupid things, and this was about as stupid as it gets.”

The TV report was playing back on a monitor which was part of an *Alan Winter Memorial Area* in an alcove near the school entrance. It had been hurriedly set up before school started with a lot of help from Cam. A large photo of Winter was draped in black and surrounded by flowers. On a table were printed flyers that contained the “facts.” There was also information about the funeral, scheduled for Thursday afternoon.

Mitch, Jordy and Amy were among the astonished students milling around, reading the handouts and watching the replay of the news report.

"Whoa!" said Mitch.

To which Jordy responded "Double whoa!"

Amy shook her head, speechless and numb. None of them had ever had a classmate die before.

Now Batt joined them, looking happy, healthy and well rested. "Nice to start the day with some good news, eh?"

"That's a sick thing to say," said Amy. "That's just sick."

"Oh, c'mon, Amy, you're not really gonna miss that asshole, are you?"

She didn't answer.

"I know *these* guys won't. Will you, guys?"

"Uh, no, I won't," admitted Jordy.

"Me neither," said Mitch.

She sighed, shook her head and walked away.

Batt shrugged. "I guess some people just don't want to admit how they feel."

Then Deuce, wearing a black armband, stepped over to Batt and whispered quietly, so quietly that neither Mitch nor Jordy could hear. "Just thought you'd like to know, dirtbag: once things settle down after the funeral? *You're history.*"

As Deuce walked away, Batt turned to Mitch and Jordy. "So, are you guys planning to go to the funeral? Pay your respects?"

Jordy snickered. “Yeah, right. How do you pay your respects when you never had any?”

“Amen,” agreed Mitch.

“True,” said Batt. “But still, it might be one to remember. That's why I'm gonna go.”

The boys looked at him in disbelief. “Really?”

Batt smiled knowingly. “Really.” And he hurried off down the hall.

***

Jordy and Mitch knew they weren't supposed to be glad that somebody died, but they certainly weren't upset about it, far from it. The TV report had called it a “Teenage Tragedy,” but they didn't think it was all that tragic. If Winter had been driving drunk and killed some innocent person, *that* would be a tragedy. But this, like the cop had said on TV, was just plain stupidity.

And yet, Mitch was bothered by something. Jordy could see it because his friend appeared to be somewhere else in the lunchroom.

“Hey, Mitch. Want some of my grapes? I'm not gonna eat 'em all.”

“Jordy? Remember when I said that sometimes I prayed that Niles and Winter and Kellie and Deuce and Cam would, like, all get killed in a car accident, or something?”

“You're not really gonna go there, are you?”

“Well, I can't help thinking about it.”

“Okay, I admit I'm thinking about it too. I prayed for the same thing. But just because Winter's dead doesn't mean God was answering our prayers.”

“But He could have been.”

“Mitch, remember what J.B. said? Actions have consequences. Well, the consequence of being an asshole, getting drunk, and climbing on a wet roof is getting killed. I mean, nobody made him drink, right? And nobody forced him to go up on the roof.”

“I guess not.”

“He made bad choices. Listen, out in the hall, I overheard Mrs. Bernstein say to Doctor Jones that it was karma.” (Mrs. Bernstein had been their English teacher last year.)

“Really? Bernstein said that?”

“Yeah. Remember, last year, when Winter put piss in her thermos and then called her a Jew bitch in front of the whole class when she found out?”

“Oh, yeah. I forgot about that.”

“So maybe it's karma for that. And for Dennis Palarin. And for Dana Madison. And for everything else he did. He did a lot of bad shit.”

“Yeah.” But Mitch didn't seem fully convinced.

“Look, Mitch, I get it that you've been feeling bad for J.B.

Me too. But Winter? Gimme a break."

"No, I don't really feel bad for him or anything. I guess it's just, I dunno, maybe I feel bad about all the bad things I wanted to happen to him. That *I'm* bad for thinking it."

"You're not bad, and you're not responsible. And I'm not responsible. And Mrs. Bernstein isn't responsible. He did this to himself, okay? I mean, we were also asking each other when do *we* get a break? Well, finally we're getting one. And I say, it's about time. Maybe that's *our* karma."

Mitch nodded, and took some of Jordy's grapes.

***

Amy was also troubled. She was troubled, not because of J.B.'s question to her about Winter's death, but because of the answer she'd been unable to give him. The truth was, she wouldn't miss Alan Winter. She wouldn't miss him sneaking into the girls' locker room, or miss him trying to peek up her skirt or miss him calling her the c-word when she wouldn't let him copy her test answers. Nor did she have any intention of attending his funeral. No, she absolutely would not miss Alan Winter, not for one single second. Yet she couldn't bring herself to say so. But why not? It wasn't like saying so meant that she thought he *deserved* to die. And it wasn't like saying so meant she was celebrating his death. Was it that she didn't want to acknowledge that there was a dark place in her soul that could entertain such thoughts? And did that mean she was a bad person? No -- she knew that even the best people sometimes had dark thoughts. Did it mean she was a hypocrite? Maybe. Maybe she was ashamed of herself for not being able to admit the truth. And maybe she felt a tinge of envy toward J.B., that he could be so honest in calling Winter's death "good news." There was something about J.B. that fascinated her. He was different from anyone she'd ever known. There was an aura of mystery around him. And, she had to admit, since his return to school yesterday, she found him somewhat attractive. So maybe *that* was what was troubling her. Regardless, she made up her mind to keep an eye on him.

***

The Funeral Chapel was filling up, but there were more adults than students. These were the friends, relatives and associates of the Winter family. The Hard Corps kids were there, as were some sycophants who came in hopes that by being there, they'd score some points with Niles (they were wrong), but that was pretty much it for the Woody High Students. Doctor Jones was the only member of the school faculty attending, and only because she felt it was part of her responsibility as principal. The truth was, none of the teachers or administrators had ever liked Alan Winter, and attending the funeral of an asshole was not in their job description.

Jordy and Mitch entered together. School had been let out early to allow students to attend the funeral, but most kids had gone home or to the mall or anywhere else. Jordy and Mitch would have gone home as well, but Batt had been adamant that they attend. Three times in three days he had urged them to attend, promising that it would be memorable, so they finally said yes. Among the ushers were Niles and Deuce, and they actually looked respectable in their dark suits and ties. They were astounded to see Mitch and Jordy enter the chapel.

"What are you stools doin' here?" whispered Niles as they walked past him.

"We wanna make sure he's really dead," Mitch told him.

"Yeah," said Jordy. "Guys who die around you seem to have a habit of coming back."

Niles gave them a look of disdain. Did they actually just sass him? Well, he'd teach them another lesson – after he took care of Batt-man.

Jordy and Mitch looked around for Batt. He wasn't here yet, so they sat in a pew off to the side, making sure to leave room for him. They were surprised when Amy walked in – they hadn't expected her to attend. She was alone, and she spotted them and she was equally surprised to see them. She sat down next to Jordy.

"What are *you* doing here?" they both whispered simultaneously, and then they both smiled.

Jordy went first. "J.B. said it'd be something to remember."

Amy nodded. “That's why I'm here too.”

“Wait – he told you too?” asked Jordy, amazed.

“No. But I overheard him say it to you guys.”

Jordy gave her a look, but she just shrugged. “Hey, I like to know what's going on, and I *know* there's something going on with J.B.”

***

The service had been going on for 40 minutes, and there was still no sign of Batt. And even though they knew it was standard procedure at all funerals, it bothered them to hear the pastor and family members say nice things about Alan Winter, because they were sure he'd never done one nice thing in his life. The pastor actually said that angels would be welcoming him to heaven, and *that* was an image that they absolutely could not get their heads around. Even Amy rolled her eyes at that one. Clearly, this pastor had never met Alan Winter.

Right now, Niles was at the pulpit, reading from a prepared speech. According to the printed order-of-the-service they'd been given, he was the last of the “tribute givers,” which had included Winter's father Bradley, his grandfather and an uncle. The boys basically paid no attention to what Niles said. Amy was bored as well.

Niles was wrapping it up. “...a great guy, a great friend, and

I'm really gonna miss him. But we can all take comfort in knowing that Alan's in a better place. Amen."

The attendees said "Amen," and Niles went back to the pew where Deuce, Kellie and Cam were seated.

The pastor returned to the pulpit. "There's one more friend of Alan's who will speak today -- he's not on your printed handout, but he came to me right before the service with such a passionate heartfelt desire to add his thoughts that I couldn't refuse. James?"

Batt stepped out from the wings, dressed in a black suit, looking very proper.

Jordy, Mitch and Amy gasped in unison.

"Whoa. This oughta be interesting," said Amy.

"Big time," said Jordy.

"Amen," said Mitch.

Closer to the front, Niles, Deuce, Kellie and Cam reacted in complete astonishment as they exchanged uncomfortable glances: w*hat on earth was* ***he*** *gonna say?*

And at the same time, Winter's parents and relatives in the front row were touched that there was another boy – someone that they'd never heard of – who wanted to remember Alan in his own way, and share it with them.

Batt stepped to the pulpit and cleared his throat. "I didn't know Alan as long as all of you. But I *did* know him long enough to get a good sense of what he was really like. As an example, in 8th grade, he and his friends took time to play basketball with the

Special Ed kids – the autistic ones who were slow to respond..."

Mr. and Mrs. Winter – Bradley and Barbara – were quite moved to hear this.

Batt continued, his voice full of admiring emotion. "Alan came up with his own special version of the game to play with these poor unfortunate children..."

Niles and Deuce exchanged a look: *how could he know this?* They slumped down a bit in their pews.

Batt continued, relating the story as if it was the most wonderful thing in the world. "He'd throw the basketball at their heads, as hard as he could, over and over, until they cried. And Alan would laugh boisterously, finding great joy in this, calling them 'You stupid spaz retards.'"

The congregation was shocked and speechless. Bradley Winter was shocked, but not speechless. He pointed an accusing finger at Batt in outrage. "Who do you think you are, demeaning my son? Show some respect for the dead!"

Batt turned his intense stare on Mr. Winter. "What about respect for the *living,* Bradley? Alan never had any. Did he ever tell you and Barbara about his first sexual experience? He and his pals – they're sitting right over there," and he pointed to Niles and Deuce, "they gang-raped a 13-year-old and put her in the hospital."

Niles and Deuce slumped lower. Niles whispered, "who told him?"

Deuce simply shrugged.

It was all too much for Bradley Winter. He jumped to his feet in rage. “Listen, you bastard, you get outta here right now or I'll teach you a lesson you'll never forget!”

“Oh, really?” Batt responded calmly. “And what'll you do, tough guy? Hit me? Like you hit your wife? Like three years ago when you hit her so hard you put her in the hospital and told everyone she slipped and fell down the stairs?”

A buzz went through the audience – many of them remembered this incident.

Bradley slowly sat back down, numb, while Barbara sobbed in anguish.

Batt kept on him. “You've got a lotta nerve talking about respect, mister wife beater. And let me tell you something else, Bradley: Contrary to what Doug just said, Alan's *not* in a better place, because God doesn't let scum into heaven. Your son will *never* rest in peace. But a lot of his classmates *will* rest easier because Alan can never hurt them again, ever. Amen.”

Jordy and Mitch looked at each other with amazement, and quietly echoed “Amen.” Amy just shook her head in open-mouthed disbelief.

“Back to you, Reverend,” said Batt as he stepped off the podium.

The pastor was every bit as stunned as everyone else. For the first time in his 28 year career, he didn't know what to say.

***

Jordy, Mitch and Amy walked out of the chapel together. They were certainly glad they attended – this had been a funeral service that no one in Westover would forget for years to come.

"Now I *really* want to find out all about your friend," Amy told them. "Will you help me, Jordy? *Please?*"

Jordy looked at her uneasily. He was starting to like her, but he still had some doubts. "Uh...well, I'd like to, only, uh, I got a lotta homework. C'mon, Mitch."

The boys took off.

Amy watched them go with a determined expression on her face. There was more to learn, much more, and somehow, she was going to find out.

Chapter 14

It was dark when Kellie got home. What a terrible afternoon. She had never thought much of Alan Winter to begin with and now, having been exposed to his family, her opinion was even lower. The funeral service had been bad enough; the graveside service was quieter, but the tension was thick, given that Bradley Winter had been exposed as a wife beater. No one even wanted to look at him. And then Doug made her go with him to the Winters' house to pay their respects, which consisted of siting around, nibbling bad food, mouthing inane pleasantries and having every adult male sneak looks at her ass and hit on her. She knew that their wives were annoyed that she wore such a short, tight, black dress to a funeral, and they weren't wrong to call it a cocktail dress – but fuck 'em all: her philosophy was to use what she had while she had it, and before she started to look like her mother. She couldn't tell if the Winters blamed Doug for Alan's death, but after what Batt-man had said, everyone was walking on eggshells. No one could say much of anything without possibly insulting someone else, so Batt was simply dismissed as a bad kid from the wrong side of the tracks who liked to make trouble. Easy to say, but as far as she could tell, everything he'd said had been true. And that was the elephant in the room that no one wanted to acknowledge. How the hell had Batt-man found out all that stuff? Was he somehow connected to the police? Maybe he had he seen some confidential hospital records. Regardless, she was glad to have taken her own car. She was getting annoyed with "The Syndicate." She'd expected bigger and better things out of Doug by now, but it was clear Doug wasn't his father, and she'd have to start seriously thinking beyond him if she expected to ascend a ladder that went higher. She already knew that high school offered only so many possibilities. Nevertheless, thanks to his father, Doug's credit card had no limit, and a girl had to look good on her way up.

Kellie lived in a boring tract house in a forgettable neighborhood. It was all that her mother could afford after her ugly divorce. Her brother Joey was in boarding school and when he wasn't, he lived with their father. The old man used his money like a weapon and had decided he'd rather pay his lawyer a whole lot more so he wouldn't have to pay his ex-wife just a little more. Kellie wanted nothing to with that sleazeball, which was about all she had in common with her mom. Her mom didn't even realize that what little they'd gotten from him was in exchange for Kellie's silence about what he'd tried to do to her one night five years ago when he came home drunk. If Joey hadn't awakened crying about a bad dream, well, things would have turned out a whole lot worse. Even Joey didn't know the whole truth; Kellie decided to reserve that card for the future.

She lit up a joint as she entered the house, and her iPhone was ringing before she could even unzip. It was her standard ringtone, which meant it wasn't Doug. She checked the display: *Unknown Caller.* She could guess who it was. “Hello?”

She heard his voice and knew she was right. “Dammit, Tommy, I left you a message: I had to go to a funeral.”

She let him rant for a bit, then interrupted. “Yeah, I know who he is, but there was nothing I could do! My boyfriend wanted me with him, and you know who his father is, right?”

Right. That usually got Tommy to calm down. She listened.

“Tomorrow night? That's Friday, so it'll have to be late. Like, 11:30 or something.” He put her on hold for a few moments, then confirmed it.

“Yeah, “ she told him, “I've got the address and I swear I won't cancel. Yeah, me too.” She ended the call and took off her jacket as she entered her bedroom.

Suddenly, the overhead light came on. She turned and gasped: Batt was standing in the doorway, still wearing the black suit he'd worn to the service.

“You look totally hot in black” he told her.

“What the hell are you doing here?” she yelled, totally outraged.

“Funerals turn me on. And I am *so* horny right now...”

She couldn't help but chortle. “Don't make me laugh, faggot.”

"And how do you know I don't go both ways?"

"You? Yeah, right. Just get out. Or I'll call Doug."

"Why not consider me a paying client?"

She froze for a moment, reacting with a guilty look. She gulped. *How much did he know?*

"Oh, I'm totally up on your little arrangement with Mr. Rayburn. Or should I say, 'Uncle Tommy?'"

Shit. "Who talked?"

He smiled. "Let's just say I travel in different circles than the rest of Woody High. But I'm sure you figured that out by now. It's six bills, right? I hope you're worth it."

"Tommy didn't set this up. He didn't say anything about it."

"Why involve 'Uncle Tommy?' If we eliminate the middle man, you get to keep it all. No 50% 'finder's fee.'"

Jeez, he knew that too. "I thought you didn't have any money."

"I lied." And he held up six, crisp new 100-dollar bills.

Her jaw dropped.

"They can all be yours, 'Miss Kellie.' It'll be our little secret."

She was on the fence...

"And I promise, I don't have that disgusting, blubbering bad breath that some of your clients have."

She reached for the bills, but he pulled them back.

"So you *do* want me to stay?"

Her demeanor did a complete 180. "As long as you like,

sweetie," she said, very agreeably.

Batt let her take the money. She put the bills in a drawer.

"So, where's your Mom?" he asked as he took off his suit coat. "She's not gonna walk in us or anything, is she?"

"No, she's with her boyfriend. In Jamaica."

"Excellent. Then we'll have plenty of time."

She snickered silently. *Yeah, right. This guy was a two-pump chump if she'd ever seen one – if he could get it up at all.*

"You don't mind if we do it with the lights on?" he asked. "I want to be able to see every inch of your gorgeous body."

Oh, puh-leeez! What stupid movie did he get that line from? "The customer is always right," she smiled.

"Then turn off your phone," he said. "I don't like to be interrupted."

She did so. *Wow. He sure has a high opinion of his prowess.*

"Now, come towards me and look into my eyes. I can learn a lot about a girl by looking into her eyes."

Cornball city. It was all she could do not to laugh, but for 600 dollars, she managed. She looked into his eyes, and then looked deeper. She suddenly found his gaze completely compelling, and she couldn't have looked away even if she had wanted to. But she didn't want to. And weird as it seemed, his irises actually appeared to be changing colors while she stared into them...

***

She gasped, exhausted. It had been her fourth orgasm in 90 minutes and she was beyond fulfilled. It was the most satisfying sexual experience she'd ever had. She'd been touched in places she didn't know could be touched, and stimulated in ways that she couldn't even describe. It was like she'd never done it right before – or that no one had ever done her right. His fingers, his tongue, his cock – they were all magic. *How was it possible – him, of all people!* Funny. Those magazines had always said that there was a difference between having sex and making love but until now, she had thought it was utter tripe. How wonderful to be wrong.

She rolled off of him. “Oh my God, that was *amazing.* Nobody's *ever* fucked me like that! Ever!”

“Not even Doug...?”

“Mr. Fast and Furious? I fake it with him. If he could do me even half as good as you just did...” She sighed with happiness. “It's like you were reading my mind. Oooo, I feel like jello...!”

Batt reached for his wallet on the nightstand. He pulled out a crisp 50-dollar bill and handed it to her somewhat theatrically. “Well, I got my money's worth. I'm a very satisfied customer.”

“Any time, baby. *Any* time.”

Batt smiled sardonically as he put on his clothes. *Tomorrow was going to be good.*

Chapter 15

It was the first juicy *Hard Woody 411* posting in over a week – the Alan Winter stuff had been boring, cloying and perfunctory – and the new edition had apparently gone online just a few minutes ago. Whatever, it was spreading like wildfire and was rocking the student body like no other posting before. Every kid with a tablet, smartphone or laptop was showing it to every other kid with or without one in the halls before school began.

The headline screamed "**50 DOLLAR WHORE!**" There was an image of Kellie and Batt in bed which, upon clicking, became motion video of Batt giving her the 50 dollar bill as he said "I got my money's worth."

"She did it for 50 bucks??" said a girl in disbelief.

"What a slut!" said another.

An iPad a few feet away played back a different moment, with Kellie saying "Mr. Fast and Furious? I fake it with him."

Kellie walked down the corridor in a state of shock. Everywhere she went, kids were playing this stuff back. To her face, she was met with calls of "Slut!" "Whore!" "Skank!" "Bitch!" "Skag!"

She ignored them.

“I'll give you 60!” said a guy.

“Do you give group rates?” asked one of the linebackers.

“How much is a blow job?” asked another.

How could Doug do this to her? She continued along, trying to hold it together. The comments behind her back were even worse.

“She must be on crack to do it for 50!” said a guy.

“And to think I let her in my house!” said Brittany Lawrence.

“I hope they disinfect the bathrooms,” said Tiffany Vandeman.

Jordy and Mitch were delighted witnesses to the abuse, and as Kellie passed them, they chimed in.

“Oh, you poor slut,” said Jordy in mock sympathy. “Is everybody talkin' about you behind your back?” And then, sharply, “What goes around comes around, *bitch*!”

“You're so foul, I wouldn't even let my dog pee on you!” Mitch called.

She just kept walking with an expression like ice. She wasn't going to give anyone the satisfaction of seeing her crack.

The boys high-fived each other, then turned and found Amy in front of them.

“You guys don't *really* believe she did J.B. for 50 bucks?” she asked.

“Who cares?” shrugged Mitch. “She's gettin' what she deserves.”

“Maybe,” Amy conceded. “But J.B. being at the center of everything, doesn't it make you wanna know who he really is?”

“Maybe,” admitted Jordy.

She moved closer to him. “So *maybe* "Buffy" and "CSI" should team up. *Maybe* "the truth is out there" and we can find it together.”

Jordy wasn't sure if it was his attraction to Amy or his curiosity about J.B. that was more enticing. He looked at Mitch, but he could see that Mitch wasn't so sure this was a good idea.

Jordy turned to Amy and tried to play it cool. “Maybe.” he offered.

***

Doug Niles walked quickly and resolutely down a different hall – he wore an intense expression and was clearly on a mission, so he ignored the snide remarks. Deuce tailed slightly, trying to keep up with him.

“Hey, it's the original 'Fast and Furious!'”

“What's she charge *you*, Dougie?”

“Do you get a 'minute-man' discount?”

“If Batt-man's a fag, what's that make you?”

Niles was seething. He had never been so dissed in his life. He turned the corner and found Kellie at her locker. It had "WHORE" spray painted on it in red. Ha. Someone had saved him the trouble.

He got right in her face. "'Fast and furious,' eh? I'll show you furious!"

He slapped her. She flinched.

"Fake *that*, you cheap slut!"

"*You're* the slut! How *dare* you put a camera in my room! Did you put one in my bathroom too? So you can jerk off to seeing me in the shower? Or show your creepy friends? I can't believe you fucking did this to me!"

"I did it to *you*? You opened your legs, you fucking donut hole! You can go to hell! You and fucking Batt-man both!"

"At least J.B's a man! Instead of a pencil dick!"

She slammed her locker and walked off in a huff.

A small crowd had witnessed this and responded with catcalls. Others had recorded the confrontation on their phones. Niles spun around and glared at them, his face bright red. "Fuck off! All of you!" But no one was intimidated. Not today.

Now a very anxious Cam came running over to Niles. "Hey, Doug, listen --"

Niles turned on him, livid. "How long have you had that camera in her room? Tell me! How long?"

"Hey, look, I didn't – "

"And how many times do I gotta tell you, don't post shit till I approve it! Surprises like this I don't need!"

Deuce got between them. "He had no choice, man! I mean,

if Batt-man started saying he fucked her for fifty, you'da torn his head off, and then you'da really looked like an asshole, defending a whore! He did you a *favor*, man! He *protected* you!"

Niles took a moment and considered this. It made sense. Sort of. "Yeah, yeah, okay, maybe so. But why'd you put that 'fast and furious' shit in there?"

Deuce answered before Cam could reply. "So that you'd know what she really thought of you! So she wouldn't be able to bullshit you about it!"

Niles gave Cam a shove. "You coulda shown it to me privately, asshole! But this is personal, ain't it? You wanted to get back at me, didn't ya?"

"No, Doug, I swear. I didn't even--"

But Niles was too pissed to keep a single thought in his head for more than a few seconds. "Goddamn that fucking slut!" he screamed. "Well, she's history now. She'll never be able to go anywhere again. Serves her right, too. But fucking Batt-man's still dead!"

The bell rang. Niles and Deuce hurried off, leaving a bewildered Cam to call after them weakly. "But I didn't do anything! I don't know who posted it!"

Chapter 16

Kellie walked intently out of the school. No way could she stay in class today. No way at all.

Fatso Evans, the school guard, spotted her. “Miss Davies! Where do you think you're going? The bell has rung.”

She kept walking.

“You cut class, you get detention, Miss Davies.”

She muttered “kiss my ass, fatso,” and kept going.

“That's it, I'm writing you up!”

She ignored him and headed for the parking lot. And in moments, she saw how quickly her fellow students could work when they were motivated. Bright red letters had been spray painted on the hood of her white Mustang. They spelled "SLUT."

She fumed, climbed into her car and peeled out.

She had no idea where she was going. Just – away. Far, far away. She rolled down the windows, blasted her music and headed west.

***

She was so numb and spaced out that she never even saw his

hand reach forward from the back seat to turn off the stereo.

“Nice friends you got,” said Batt.

She gasped, freaked, and almost lost control of the car.

“Jesus fucking Christ” she shouted. “You've been back there the whole time?”

“Duh.”

“What do you want, you bastard? This is all your fault, you know that?”

“What, you think *I* posted it? I wouldn't even know how. Besides, you're the career girl. But don't worry, I know how to fix it.”

“Fuck you, liar! You just ruined my life, you son of a bitch! I don't wanna have anything else to fucking do with you!”

“Okay, fine,” said Batt. “I'm a liar and I can't fix it. Pull over, I'll get out, and you can go through life, knowing they'll *always* call you a whore and whisper behind your back and post that video wherever you go. It'll be on Facebook. And YouTube. And Vimeo. And Daily Motion. And every other website. And a zillion blogs. No matter where you go, it'll be there for people to find. When they google 'Kellie Davies,' it'll be the first thing that comes up. But you ain't no Kardashian, and your mom's no Kris Jenner. So pull over, and I'll walk away and say welcome to the rest of your life.”

But she didn't pull over. He knew she wouldn't. She kept driving.

And after a long silence, she spoke. “All right, how can you fix it?”

“Turn right,” he told her. “Down that road.”

She turned right at the intersection and he climbed into the front. They were now heading down a semi-rural road and it looked like there might be construction ahead.

“First,” he said, “you promise that all your dissing, ripping and harassment stops. Of anyone and everyone.”

“Okay, okay, and then what?”

“Then I fess up. I go in front of the school and say that the whole thing was faked -- we never really did anything. I'll say I hacked the *Hard Woody* website and posted it as a class project -- to show how quickly we're ready to believe the worst about someone who's entirely innocent. It's why we have to put an end to *Hard Woody 411*. And it'll really rip Niles and them. Then, everyone'll start backpedaling and fawning and kissing your ass. You'll be untouchable.”

Her face brightened as she realized it could actually work.

“That's brilliant. It's *perfect!* Oh, I can't wait to hear their excuses. It'll be epic. I'll *own* them. I'll own them all! J.B., you are so smart! I wanna do you. I want your beautiful fat cock in me right now! Let's seal it with a fuck!”

“Okay, okay, but stop for a second – I gotta pee.”

She pulled over and put the car in park. Batt got out.

She sat back, sighed with relief, and smiled with anticipation.

"Yeah, Doug's gonna be history. It'll be so-ooo great!"

Batt closed the car door and stuck his head through the open window.

"Hey. Remember when you lied to Mitch about really wanting to save his dog? Well, I just lied to you about really wanting to save your rep. I don't. And I *did* post that video. You're done, slut."

She looked at him with shock.

He smiled, stepped back, and made a small downward gesture with his index and middle fingers. *The car doors locked by themselves.*

He made a circular gesture with the same two fingers: *the engine revved!*

He shook his head. "Teenage suicide. So sad."

He made another gesture, pulling his fist toward himself. *The shift lever popped into Drive all by itself! The car roared off!*

"Enjoy the ride, bitch."

Kellie's eyes widened in horror. *What the hell was happening???* She pumped the brake pedal – harder -- harder – but the car kept accelerating! She tried to shift out of Drive, but she couldn't – it was jammed! *Holy shit!*

She looked ahead – there was some heavy excavation equipment on the right side of the road, just before the bend, and her car was heading directly toward it!

She frantically jerked the steering wheel – but it wouldn't

budge!

Batt watched with amusement, imagining the fear she was feeling.

Kellie's panic increased. She tried to open the door – she couldn't! She tried to turn off the ignition -- she couldn't!

Her speedometer needle passed 40...

She reached out the open window and tried to open the door from the outside -- but it wouldn't open!

She looked in terror at the Excavator looming larger: it was the meanest looking piece of construction equipment she'd ever seen – full of hard blades and spikes, 30 tons worth! She was going to be dead in moments, unless –

One chance: she started climbing out her open window!

Batt's expression abruptly changed: *no!* He wasn't expecting this. He gestured with his fingers, but nothing happened – she was out of range!

The speedometer needle passed 45 and she was halfway out the window.

The highway below her was a whooshing blur. Hitting it was going to hurt, but what choice did she have? She looked ahead: The Excavator was only seconds away.

She grimaced and forced herself out the window and --

She hit the pavement at 49 miles per hour and bounced forward as --

IMPACT! The Mustang slammed into the Excavator at 50

miles per hour and exploded in a tremendous fireball!

Kellie, bruised and bloody, screamed, writhing in pain on the pavement, with fiery debris near her.

Batt was pissed – he had fucked up royally. She was alive! How did he not remember to roll up the windows? Damn, if she lived through this... Well, he didn't want to think about *that*. He still had time. He should be able to do something.

Kellie struggled to crawl clear of the fire. Then, suddenly from around the bend, a huge 18-Wheeler thundered through and *ran right over her*, smashing her bloody, mangled body to a pulp!

Batt sighed relief and smiled. "Never mind. That's two...!"

Chapter 17

Amy had decided it was best for her to go to Jordy's house for several reasons. First, he'd be more comfortable on his own turf. Second, it ensured he wouldn't get cold feet and not show up at her house – boys were notoriously unreliable -- and she'd also been concerned Mitch might talk him out of it. And third, she had a car and he didn't, and it'd be a long bike ride for him. She lived a mile north of school and he lived on the south end of town. No point in making this more difficult for him, given his general reluctance.

She had gone home after school to get her MacBook and some cables. Jordy said he had DSL with a wi-fi router, but she wanted to be prepared. By the time she'd gotten organized and found his house, Mitch was already there. He'd brought his dog along and the beagle was not only incredibly adorable, but brought out a warmth and kindness in Mitch that she'd never observed before. She'd never had much of a sense of him and had only ever thought of him as an unjust victim of The Syndicate's abuse. The dog ratcheted her opinion of him up several notches. It didn't hurt that Bagel liked her too, and that made Mitch like her a little more as well.

Jordy was more computer savvy than she expected – he even

knew about spokeo.com – and before long, their computers were hooked up in tandem and they were searching the internet for some mention of J.B.

They tried several search engines, and several variations of his name. They got plenty of hits, but they all resulted in dead ends.

“That's not the Batt that you're looking for,” said Mitch, doing a pretty good Obi-Wan Kenobi impression.

Jordy sighed. “Who knew there'd be so many people named Batt?”

“C'mon,” she said, “you guys must know *something* about him that'll narrow this search. A middle name? His last school? A birthday?”

“Hey --” Mitch remembered, “he said something about New Jersey, didn't he?”

“Yeah!” exclaimed Jordy. “Trenton! That's where he got knifed!”

Amy input the new parameters, pointed, clicked, and then...

They all reacted with amazement.

“Whoa,” said Mitch. “It's him!”

The computer screen displayed a Trenton news article: ***Local Youth Slain In Teen "Prank."*** Accompanying it was a photo of J.B., looking almost exactly like he did on the first day he came to school. Below, he was identified as *Arthur Jamison Battaglia, 17.*

“So he's actually Arthur Jamison? And Batt is short for

Battaglia," said Jordy. "No wonder we couldn't find him."

But Amy was more perturbed by something else. "Guys," she said with trepidation, "I know it *looks* like him, but this article's eight years old, and he looks exactly the same! If it *was* him, he'd have aged! It says he's 17, and the J.B. we know is definitely not 25."

"Angels don't age" said Mitch authoritatively.

She guffawed. "Angels?? Gimme a break!"

"Remember the funeral?" said Mitch. "How'd he know all that stuff about Winter and his old man? How'd he know when to show up last Friday and throw that knife? How else could he come back from the dead?"

"Or suddenly show up here, just at the right moment?" said a familiar voice.

The three turned around, startled: *J.B. was standing in the doorway and he wasn't smiling.* He'd entered so quietly that not even Bagel had reacted.

"Or do this..." Batt continued, stepping into the room. He gestured at the window: the blinds dropped down by themselves and closed shut!

"Or this..."

He made another gesture over his shoulder at the door behind him, without even looking at it -- it closed automatically and locked itself!

Batt sighed. "You had to find out, didn't you? You had to

keep poking around when I told you to back off. You just wouldn't trust me."

Jordy, Mitch and Amy were very uneasy as Batt approached. They dropped their heads.

Batt shook his head and looked at the boys with disappointment. "Jordan Thomas Hubbard. Mitchell William Simon. Two more males, seduced by an "Eve" with an Apple..."

The boys exchanged guilty looks.

"No," said Jordy, "it wasn't Mitch. It was me. I'm to blame."

"But he's here too," said Batt, indicating Mitch. "He came. Didn't you, Mitch?"

Mitch nodded, ashamed of himself.

"Look," said Amy, "I was really the one who--"

"You shut up," Batt told her sharply. "You've done enough. Too much. You have *no idea* what you might have done. No fucking idea. Actions have consequences."

Amy gulped. So did the boys. No one said anything.

Batt sighed. He was clearly troubled. "Well," he said, "you wanna know so bad, I'll tell you. But just remember what they say about curiosity..."

Batt took a deep breath, then hesitated, almost as if he wasn't sure if he should proceed. "Once, I was just like you guys: harassed, constantly. But worse, more vicious. It wasn't just 'faggot, homo, assface, penis breath.' They beat me up. They busted my stuff. Put shit in my food. Made me sick. I had to wear a tube on my dick under my pants to pee into a flask around my leg because I couldn't go to the bathroom alone 'cause somebody would always jump me. And it was just me, by myself. I never had a friend. Not one. No one to talk to. No one to share the pain with. No one to even try to understand. Not even a dog. Well, I decided to do something about it. I decided to take the three bastards out. I was gonna blow up their car with all of 'em in it."

Jordy, Mitch and Amy listened, mesmerized. This kid had a major dark streak in him, and his darkness seethed from every pore.

Batt picked up a toy car from a shelf and held it up.

"I wasn't just thinkin' to do it, I was *gonna* do it. I actually built a small bomb with a detonator that would explode the gas tank."

He made a gesture with his left index finger and the toy car blew apart in his hand with a small fireball!

Jordy, Mitch and Amy gasped. Even Bagel whimpered.

Batt picked up a Batman action figure and examined it as he continued. "But I never got it hooked up. See, they killed me before I got the chance. They didn't even know what I was planning. They killed me for sport -- one of their "games" that went too far. And I went to Hell."

Batt pointed at the Batman figure and it burst into flames! In a moment, it was completely charred.

The mouths of the three listeners dropped open in unified

astonishment, both at what Batt just did and at what he just said.

He looked knowingly at their expressions of disbelief. “Oh, yeah, Hell is *real*. And it's far worse than you can possibly imagine. So think about this shit: Me, the victim, *I* went to Hell. And why? Because I was *planning* a multiple murder. Intent, but not the deed. Just like it says in the Bible, "he who has committed sin in his heart..." Yeah, I committed the murders in my heart and I was trying make 'em real. But they never happened. Well, I screamed bloody murder. I was the *victim*, not the perp. It wasn't fair that I should be dead and about to suffer eternal damnation while they were all alive. Alive with the power to turn their lives around. Alive with the ability to repent and be forgiven. So I made a proposal to The Boss – well, two of his lieutenants, actually, nobody sees The Boss. 'Send me back, as an avenger,' I told 'em. 'Let me bring you the souls of those three assholes and others like 'em before they can repent.' 'Cause if you die unrepentant, with darkness in your soul, it's hell – as I learned. So my idea was, I wouldn't give anyone a chance to clean up their act. I would bring dark, swift retribution on the scum of the earth. That's what I proposed. And they said, basically, okay, sure. But no *swift* retribution. No, if I was gonna do this for them, I had to make it interesting. Or entertaining. Or ironic. Or memorable. Entertainment for the Hell Cable Network, seven billion channels. Like, if a bad guy gets hit by a car out of nowhere without knowing why – that wouldn't cut it. No, the cat has to play with the mouse before he kills it. The mouse has to be scared. It has to squirm. Which means, all this, these past few days, has been playtime."

"Whoa," said Mitch.

"Double whoa," said Jordy.

"So here I am. With special powers that work within a radius of about 50 feet. The irony is, I never got payback on those fuckers who did me. One of 'em committed suicide. The other two got religion. Bastards. That's why my little game is designed to keep the scum off balance so they never get religion. I only get a few days, so I have to be clever. And careful. If I make a mistake and take out somebody who isn't supposed to go south, it's game over for me. Now, I truly *have* earned my place in hell. But as long as I deliver my quota, I'll never have to go."

"Quota?" said Jordy. "You mean they tell you how many souls you have to bring in?"

"No," answered Batt, "*you* do. Your prayers were heard. You said five, remember? Well, it's two down, three to go: Kellie's "suicide" was... glorious."

The boys looked at each other in stunned disbelief, not sure if they should be happy or horrified.

But Amy was completely horrified. "She's dead? Kellie Davies is *dead*?"

"Yep. So sad," Batt replied sarcastically. "Another teenager driven to suicide by malicious internet postings and vicious gossip. Oh, I fucked with her head six ways to Sunday. And her body too. Talk about irony – she got a little taste of heaven before she got served up on a platter at the inferno buffet and pig roast."

Mitch smiled with twisted delight. "Epic! So there actually *is* justice!"

Batt nodded. "Yeah. Go figure. There's no justice in America, but there's justice in hell."

It all sounded good to Jordy, too. "So can we watch? When the others go down? Can we help?"

"No! You guys stay out of this! You know way too much, and that could be very dangerous -- for all of us. I've only got till midnight tonight, so I can't let my plans get messed up. And despite what you're thinking, I *do* mess up sometimes. Just like I did in life. I almost messed up with Kellie today. She almost survived.

"Then that's exactly why we *should* help you," pleaded Mitch, "so you don't mess up!"

"Yeah!" agreed Jordy. "We could, like, make sure you have a backup plan!"

"NO!" screamed Batt, intense and resolute. He took a breath. "Believe me, you do not want to be part of this. Three people have to die tonight. For all our sakes, let's hope it's the right three."

It sounded like a threat. Mitch, Jordy and Amy exchanged uneasy looks.

"I'll catch you before I leave. So be good." And with that,

Batt turned and gestured: the door unlocked, opened by itself, and he departed.

***

The three were speechless for a few moments. And then they were speechless for a few more moments. And then they were speechless for a few more moments after that. And then Jordy and Mitch looked at each other with relief. They realized that their prayers had been answered and that at long last, their torment was about to end forever. They smiled. And they high-fived each other.

"Yes!"

Amy was appalled. "No! You guys are sick! I mean, this is all twisted and perverse and unbelievable, and, like, this is *okay* with you? You're gonna just let him kill the rest of 'em?"

"Why not?" answered Jordy. "They been asking for it." He raised the blinds and looked out the window. There was no sign of J.B.

"I'll tell you why not," she said. "Because it's *wrong*, that's why not!"

"Easy for you to say," Mitch told her. "They don't torture *you*. They don't call *you* names and humiliate you and make your life a living nightmare. They don't put pictures of you on Hard Woody 411 and make it impossible for you to have any friends."

Mitch was letting it all out. "They don't smack you upside the head on the school bus, or hip check you in the halls or try to drown you in the toilet." He picked up Bagel and caressed him gently. "And they didn't try to kill your dog." His eyes were full of tears, and it was all he could do to stop from crying. "You don't cry yourself to sleep every night, and wish that you never wake up and then get sick to your stomach when you do. You don't go to church and ask God what you've done to deserve this and never get an answer, and then go back to school on Monday and suffer again. *That's* wrong. And if they're all going to hell because of it, I'm glad. I'm really glad. Because they *do* deserve it." And he crushed what was left of the charred Batman figure.

Amy sighed. Whoa. She'd had no idea what his life was like. This poor kid really had suffered. Both of them. And it was hard to argue with his logic. Even she was hard pressed to think of anything positive to say about Doug Niles. But Niles wasn't the only target. "Well, Steve Cameron's not really a bad guy. I've known him, like, forever. He's always been nice to me."

"Yeah, and I bet Hitler was nice to his mother," snapped Jordy. "So what? So what if he's nice to you? Big fuckin' deal. I mean, if Cam's such a great guy, why does he hang with Niles? Why does he hurt us?"

"I think inside he knows it's wrong."

"If he knows it's wrong and he does it anyway, that makes him worse!" said Mitch.

Amy sighed. Again, it was logic that was hard to refute. And Steve Cameron had become a jerk. Amy silently packed up her computer. It was all too overwhelming. She needed to think this through. “I'm going home now.”

Jordy and Mitch exchanged a troubled look. She didn't get it. How could she? She didn't suffer. She didn't live their lives. And she sure wasn't at The Cabin on Friday night. So, as she stepped out the front door and headed toward her VW Beetle, the boys and Bagel followed her.

“Amy: they killed J.B.,” Jordy reminded her. “You kill somebody, you get the death penalty.”

“But they *didn't* kill him. He was already dead!”

“They didn't know that. They meant to kill him. They thought they did. And then they covered it up. No remorse. No guilt. They claimed he deserved it. We were there. We saw it. Not just the five of 'em, there were 25 other kids there. And every one of 'em stabbed J.B. and whooped and hollered and laughed it up and agreed to shut up about it. They didn't go to the cops. They didn't report it. Not one of 'em.”

Mitch picked up Bagel and held him up in front of her. “They'da killed my best little friend, Amy. They had him hanging in a noose, choking. An innocent little dog and they were gonna let him die and then laugh about it. As far as I'm concerned, his life's worth 10 times more than all theirs put together.”

“And you guys prayed for this? For all of 'em to die?”

“No,” answered Jordy, “we prayed for 'em to stop hurting us. To be punished. And we prayed to God. Only somehow, it was J.B. who was listening. So if they all end up dead because of it, I say good riddance. Maybe that was God's plan all along and He had to work through J.B. to do it. They're bad guys, Amy. You heard J.B. at the funeral. They raped a little girl. Probably ruined her life. And Dana Madison tried to kill herself because of what they did to her. And Dennis Palarin has a permanently dislocated jaw. So if you feel sorry for any of 'em for even one second, *you're* sick. If it wasn't for J.B, they mighta killed me or Mitch. You think about that.”

Amy opened her car door. “I don't know what to think. I honestly do not know how to deal with this. Y'know, before today, I wasn't even sure I believed in God. But now? I'm scared. I mean, Hell is a real place and three people are gonna die tonight and go there, and you want me to just turn my back on that and let it happen? I'm not sure I can do that.”

She climbed into her front seat and started the engine.

“Just stay out of it, Amy,” said Jordy. “Let things run their course. It'll all be over by midnight.”

“Yeah,” added Mitch. “'Cause if you tell, they'll probably take it out on us! You want *that* on your conscience?”

Amy looked away, closed her eyes, took a deep breath, then put the car in gear and drove off.

The boys sighed in unison as they watched her disappear

around the corner.

"Hey, Jordy? I – uh – I don't really wanna go home tonight."

"That's good, because I don't wanna be alone tonight either. We got some food in the freezer I can nuke."

"Well, I'm not actually very hungry."

"No, me neither."

They headed back toward the house.

"Geez," said Mitch, "I hope J.B. doesn't mess up."

"Geez," said Jordy, "I hope *I* didn't mess up by letting her talk me into this."

"Amen," replied Mitch.

And Bagel barked in agreement.

Chapter 18

Amy canceled her movie plans with Katie, Leslie and Elaine as soon as she got home, texting them, “can't make it, long story, details later.” And then she did something she hadn't done in a long time. She turned off her phone. The last thing she needed right now was to be distracted by texts, tweets, posts and instagrams about things that would make no difference tonight, tomorrow, or probably ever. She had to think.

When Amy's parents asked her at dinner why she seemed so troubled, she said it was because of a boy. It wasn't exactly a lie, and her mother nodded knowingly. Amy picked at her food, excused herself and then went to her room. “If you'd like to talk about it – him – I'm here for you, sweetie,” said her mother.

Yeah, right. There was no one Amy could talk to about this. No one. Who would believe it? Not her mother or her father. Certainly not Katie or Leslie or Elaine. Not even Carole would believe it and she believed that vampires were real and were actually aliens living among us, feeding off the human race. The truth was, Amy was having a hard enough time believing it herself. What was that line from that Kevin Spacey movie that her Dad liked so much? *The greatest trick the devil ever played was convincing the world he didn't exist.* It was one of those lines that stuck with you. And clearly, it was true. Other than Jordy, Mitch and J.B., there was no one she knew who believed in the devil as an actual being. And they probably hadn't believed in him before all of this either. In all her years of attending Sunday school, the devil had never been mentioned as a concrete entity, only metaphorically. And, although she wasn't much of a church-goer, she'd never heard hell mentioned a real place in any sermon. Her parents had never discussed Satan or hell. No, she'd always thought that literally believing in the devil and hell was restricted to ignorant people, superstitious people -- the kind of people who believed that a black cat was bad luck or a rabbit's foot brought good luck. Yet here was a truth staring her right in the face, a plain simple truth, a truth so simple that most people dismissed it. There really was Right and Wrong. God and the devil. Heaven and Hell. Actions have consequences. Bad behavior is punished. It was, she had to admit, comforting.

And yet...

And yet, she now had to make a choice. A moral decision. How was *she* going to behave? And how would her choice, her behavior, her actions -- knowing what she now knew -- ultimately be judged?

The easiest thing would be to say nothing and do nothing. It really wasn't any of her business. She was an outsider in the matter, not directly involved. Only she *was* involved. That had been her choice, to become involved, and she couldn't undo it, or pretend that she was ignorant. People would die tonight if she did nothing. Although, if she understood J.B. correctly, people would die tonight anyway. It would be a question of *who* would die. But that was assuming that J.B. was telling the truth. Could an agent of the devil even be trusted? Maybe no one would die. Maybe this all some sort of test for *her.*

And yet...

No. This couldn't be about her, it wasn't possible. It was about Mitch and Jordy. What was the right thing for *them?* She had seen the anguish in Mitch's face. In Jordy's too, but especially in Mitch. That poor kid had nothing and no one, no one except his little dog and Jordy. She had never befriended him or had said more than a few words to him. But Jordy had. By that standard, Jordy was a much better person than she was. And she couldn't forget what Mitch had said about what his life was like. It was an unending nightmare, of that she had no doubt. There was no reason that Niles and the other kids picked on him, no reason at all, and if Niles survived, she had no doubt he would continue to terrorize both Mitch and Jordy. So maybe... Maybe Niles deserved the worst.

And yet...

And yet who was she to judge? She didn't know anything about Niles's life or what made him the way he was. But did that even matter? He had done too many things that were inexcusable, no matter what the circumstances. That was a judgment that was easy to make. If it boiled down to right and wrong, Niles was wrong, with a capital W. But did he deserve the death penalty?

She turned it over in her head, backward, forwards, sideways and upside down. She went through every permutation, and then she went through them all again. *Man, this was tough.*

And so she did something else that she hadn't done in a very long time. She prayed. She got down on her knees, next to her bed, just as she'd done every night before she went to bed when she was a little girl, and she prayed. "God," she said, "help me. Help me know what's right. Help me decide what to do. Show me the way. Give me a sign." She stayed there, on her knees, waiting, contemplating, hoping. Hoping for an epiphany. Hoping for a sign. Hoping for an answer. But none came. She certainly knew why. God didn't work that way. She wasn't a puppet under God's control. Or under the devil's control. It had to be *her* choice, *her* decision. Not God's, and not anyone else's.

She sighed. She looked at the clock in her bedroom. It was almost 8:30 and she knew she couldn't put it off any longer. So she admitted to herself what she'd known for the last 45 minutes: that whatever she decided, she was going to have to live with it for the rest of her life. And that's what helped her decide. She decided that she couldn't just "let things run their course." She decided that she couldn't simply do nothing. She decided that she had to act on the information she had and give fair warning, even to guys she couldn't stand. Because if she didn't and if they died tonight, then she could never hold herself blameless.

***

She had the student roster in her iPhone, so she turned it on, ignored the 18 text messages that had accumulated, accessed the list, scrolled through the names and found “Niles, Doug.” But what was she going to say to him exactly? She had never once called him, talked to him or texted him. Nor vice versa. So why would he pay any attention to her now? He wouldn't. No, if she was going to do this, she had to do her best. She scrolled up and highlighted "Cameron, Steve." His picture came up with his number. Of course it did, Cam would have made sure that his picture was in there. Amy stared at his face. She remembered going to his birthday party when he was 13. That was ages ago, when he was a nice, harmless goofball. She sighed and entered her text message: “Have critical info about Batt. Must see you asap.” She took a deep breath and hit “send.”

Now it was up to him. And all she could do was wait.

***

The six minutes it took for him to respond felt like an eternity. But the response came and it was simply one word: WHERE?

Where, indeed? The last thing she wanted was for them to come to her house, especially not if J.B. was tailing them. No, it had to be some place neutral, a place reasonably public, but a place where she wouldn't be seen by any of her friends. She figured that no one she knew would be buying pet supplies at 8:30 on a Friday night, so she texted back, “Petco Parking Lot. Bring Niles.”

His response was quick. “15 minutes.”

So that was it. In 15 minutes, she would lay it all out for them. And then her conscience would be clear. God help her.

Chapter 19

They gathered in the Petco Parking Lot, a good 50 yards from the store, under the bright, yellowish sodium vapor lights. They were far enough from the store and the other cars that no one could hear their conversation, but close enough so that if Amy called out for help, the store's security guard would hear. Amy had arrived first and had chosen the spot with all of that in mind. But once Niles had gotten out of his BMW and looked at her with his sneer of disdain, she realized that her fears were groundless: he clearly had zero interest in her either as a human being or as a sex object.

The guys had all come in separate cars -- Deuce in a Trans-Am and Steve Cameron in his RAV4. Whatever they'd been doing, they hadn't been doing it together. Or maybe they had, and were planning on going somewhere else separately. Whatever. They were guys, they were always doing stuff that made no sense, and besides, none of that mattered to Amy. What mattered was what they would do now that she'd told them what they were up against.

They'd already heard about Kellie's suicide and weren't disturbed by it. "Yeah, so the bitch killed herself, serves her right. So what?" said Niles.

But the idea that Batt had made it happen was beyond

ridiculous to them. "He told you that? What a crock! Just makes me hate him even more."

And Niles's reaction to the rest of the story was predictable. "Eat me, bitch, that's the lamest shit I ever heard!"

Deuce blew two cigarettes' worth of smoke in her face. "Like, you think you're gonna scare us with some stupid hell and damnation crap? I mean, who died and made you a fucking nun?"

She blew his smoke back at him. "Hey, you're in danger. If you don't wanna believe it, don't believe it. But I'm telling you, it's true."

Niles snickered. "Yeah, right. Batt-man's the devil. And Wheezer's the Tooth Fairy and Shrimpboat's the fucking Easter Bunny. I'm so-o-o-o scared. So who put you up to this, bitch? Batt-man? Or the stool samples?"

She hadn't finished what she'd planned to say, and she could see it was pointless to even try. Instead, she gave Niles a look, turning her nose at the stench of liquor on his breath. "Actually, they told me to stay away from you."

"Guess they're gettin' some brains in their old age. Well, go tell 'em that we laughed. Or, just stick around and suck our cocks. Since Kellie's not around, old jumbo's gettin' lonely!" Niles grabbed his crotch and made some obscene gestures. Deuce did the same and cackled.

Amy rolled her eyes. Niles and Deuce weren't just degenerate assholes, they were pathetic degenerate assholes. She looked over at Cam who had been completely silent both during and after her explanation. He met Amy's gaze for only an instant before he looked away.

She looked back at Niles and Deuce. "Maybe Jordy was right about you guys. Maybe you *do* deserve it." She shrugged. "Well, I'm done. Message delivered. The rest is on you. Go to hell. You'll be in good company."

She got back in her VW Bug and drove off.

Deuce spat. "Fucking cunt."

Niles glared at Cam. "What the fuck, Cam? Makin' us come over here for this stupid Bible thumpin' sermon shit?"

"Hey, I didn't know what she had in mind, Doug! I thought maybe she had something on him we oughta know!"

Deuce blew another cloud of smoke. "She had a crock is what she had! Filled to the brim with fucking diarrhea."

Cam wasn't so sure it was a crock. "Only, what if she's right, man? What if he's really not human?"

"Fuck me, you watch too many Zombie shows. This ain't The Walking Dead."

"Didn't you hear her? This *isn't* some zombie shit. Why couldn't he really be, like, the Angel of Death or something?"

"Angel of Death my ass."

"But in church they told us that – "

Niles got right in his face. "Fuck church, man! Church is run by faggots who do little boys! Don't believe *nothin*' you hear in church. Church is totally fucked up!"

"Amen," echoed Deuce.

Niles took a pull on his flask and lit a cigarette. And then he grinned. "You know what? You did okay, Cam. This is good fucking news. The fact that they sent her over here to try to spook us means Batt's really scared. And he *should* be. Because check out what I just borrowed from my old man's house..."

Niles popped his trunk. Along with a flashlight and some tools was an attache case. Niles opened it. Inside were two handguns. "9 millimeter Glocks. Full clips, 15 shots. "

"All right!" exclaimed Deuce.

Cam's response was a somewhat stunned "Jeez. And, like, your old man loaned 'em to you?"

"Fuck no! That dumb ass is so clueless, he doesn't even know I know about 'em."

Deuce reached for one, but Niles knocked his arm away. "Not here, dipshit! There's a guard at the store."

"Oh, yeah. Sorry."

"Tonight," proclaimed Niles, "we avenge Winter. Tonight finish it. We finish off Batt-man and both his fuckin' fag 'Robins.' And we're gonna make it look like a suicide pact."

Deuce cackled. Cam gulped.

***

The house at 4377 Glasser Road was totally dark. There were no lights, no activity, and no vehicles in front or in the driveway -- the entire block was dark and quiet. It was a part of town that had few street lights. The moon, 4 nights past full, provided what light there was.

Cam drove his RAV4 down the street at about 10 miles per hour, then slowed in front of the house, stopped for a few seconds, then continued and turned the corner. Moments later, Niles followed in his Beemer and did the same thing. And then, some 15 seconds later, Deuce drove up, slowed, and turned the corner as well.

They parked in front of a vacant lot about a half block away and gathered by Niles's car, keeping their voices down.

“You sure that's his house, man?” Deuce asked Cam skeptically.

“I hacked the school computer. That's what came up.”

“Okay,” said Niles, “me and Deuce'll stake it out. You track down Shrimpboat and Wheezer. If Batt-man comes home alone, we'll nail him here. If he's with them, text me and we'll all take care of the three of 'em.”

“Yeah, okay.”

“And if he ain't with the stools, stake 'em out and text us if he shows.”

“Got it.”

“And Cam? Tonight, no recording. *Nothing*.”

"I knew that."

Cam got back in his car and drove off.

"My car," Niles told Deuce. "Yours stinks."

Deuce rode bitch and Niles drove around the block and parked on Glasser, about a half block from 4377, in a good stakeout position to see the house.

Deuce lit up a pair of cigarettes.

"Don't get your fucking ashes on the seat this time."

"Yeah, yeah, yeah."

***

Cam didn't go far. He turned another corner, then pulled over, grabbed his Galaxy 4 and texted Amy. "*Need to talk. Just you and me. Meet me at Denny's?*"

Her response came back quickly. "*OK. 10 minutes.*"

***

They were both drinking coffee, but Cam was so jittery, he didn't really need the caffeine. Nor did he need the five packs of sugar he'd dumped into it. She told him everything, everything she had wanted to tell them all before. And what she told him, and the way she told him, only made him more jittery. He had to put the cup down because he couldn't hold it without shaking.

"Damn! I *knew* it wasn't bullshit!"

"And it wasn't just because of the things he did," she continued. "When he told us, his voice, it, like, cut right through me -- I got chills, like when you know something is totally true."

"Yeah. I kinda got chills when you were tellin' us. I think I sorta knew even before.

I mean, Winter said it was a trick knife and blood bags in his shirt, but that was no trick knife. It went in him. There weren't any blood bags. It cut him. *I* cut him. I cut his leg. Blood came out. He was dead. We carried the body. He was *dead.* I haven't slept right since. Nightmares every night. I'm a mess."

Cam was physically shaking. He closed his eyes and grabbed the table to steady himself. It took him a full 30 seconds to regain some sense of composure.

"What happened to you, Steve? You're not like Niles. You used to be okay. I mean, you used to write poems. You did math tutoring. I used to like you."

"Yeah?"

She nodded. "And don't you have a dog?"

"Inky. Scottish terrier."

"But you were gonna let Mitch's dog die?"

"No, I wasn't! I swear I wasn't! I'da done something to stop it."

She gave him that same look that her father gave her whenever she was on extremely thin ice. The bullshit detector look.

Cam sighed. Busted. He dropped his head. "Okay, I dunno what I woulda done. It was, like, totally surreal that night. And I thought – I thought as long as I was Cam the cameraman, looking at the display, it wasn't real and, like, I wasn't really part of it."

"And that gang rape? You were part of that too?"

"No! I mean, like, yeah, I heard about it, but I wasn't there -- I swear!"

Amy believed him. "But you didn't do anything. You didn't report it."

Cam shook his head in shame.

They were both silent for a while. And then Cam sighed. It was time to confess.

"Look, Amy, the truth is, well, Niles, he basically, y'know, he bought me off. He decided he wanted to do all this video and computer and internet stuff, except he didn't know how; he needed an expert. So I figured if I did it for him, I'd be safe, y'know? Instead of bein' like, just a techno geek, I'd be one of the Syndicate. I know Niles is an asshole, but he's King Shit, and when you hang with the king, nobody fucks with you."

"And that's the point of everything? That's the meaning of life? That nobody fucks with you?"

Cam shrugged. "It's better than bein' fucked *with*."

"Well, now you're fucked *up*. Big time."

He looked at her in anguish. "So, what do I do? I mean,

like, Batt's really comin' after me?"

"That's what he said."

"How do I stop him? How do I fix it?"

She shook her head. "No idea. But even if I *did* know? It wouldn't matter. Because if there *is* an answer, whatever it is, it's gotta come from you." And with that, she got up and left.

Steve Cameron was devastated. No, actually, he was more than devastated. He was fucked. He checked his phone: 10:14. So he had less than two hours to get himself un-fucked.

Chapter 20

Niles and Deuce were bored out of their minds, staring at the moonlit dark house and smoking. They couldn't even play any music. Neither had much to say to the other. Then again, they never did.

Niles's iPhone said it was 10:33. He texted Cam.

"*Anything?*"

The response came back quickly. "*No sign of B Man yet.*"

"This is getting fucking old," complained Deuce. "I want some action."

As if in response, a light came on in an upstairs window. Niles pointed it out to Deuce. "Looks like he heard ya."

They moved quietly, taking care not to slam the car doors. Niles popped the trunk. They each took a Glock and shoved it into their waistbands. Niles grabbed the flashlight and a screwdriver, then quietly closed the trunk.

"You gonna text Cam?" whispered Deuce.

"No, fuck him. We can handle this. He'll just whine and get in the way."

Niles didn't even lock the car for fear that the squeal of the alarm arming might alert Batt they were here. They crept down the street, past three dark houses, to number 4377 and entered the property, ignoring a "No Trespassing" sign in the front yard. The sign hadn't been there last week when the house last had visitors, and if Niles and Deuce had bothered to read it, they might have noticed that the next line read, "Violators Subject To Termination." But it wouldn't have changed anything – they were going in.

Just like Jordy and Mitch, they went around back. The window pane in the back door was no longer broken. Niles tried the door. It opened.

Once inside, Niles played the flashlight beam over the dilapidated environment. A roach sprinted across a counter top, and that was the only sign of habitation they found. "Jeez. What kinda fucked up fucker lives in a fucked up shit hole like this?" whispered Deuce.

Niles's light illuminated a familiar DayGlo purple binder. He smiled.

"The kind of fucker who owns that fucked up binder, that's who. Let's find the stairs."

They moved cautiously and quietly into the next room. Their eyes were adjusting to the darkness. In front of them was the staircase. Their destination was upstairs.

***

Cam hadn't actually gone to Jordy's house, but there was no

reason for Niles to know that. And there was certainly no reason for Niles to know where he had just been, or where he was going. *Church.* His Google Maps app told him there were six churches within a one-mile radius. Cam had now been to five of them, and they were all closed. Apparently, Cam concluded, God kept hours and had gone home early. The Westover Methodist Church was his last hope, but that hope vanished as Cam drove up to it. It was dark, just like the others, and there were no cars in the parking lot. Still, he was here, so he decided to make sure. He parked, jogged up the front steps and tried the front door. Locked.

He checked his phone. 10:45. He sighed hopelessly, sat down on the church steps and dropped his head in his hands. And then, after feeling sorry for himself, he did something he hadn't done in a very long time. He prayed. He got down on his belly and prayed for guidance and hoped that God really didn't keep hours.

***

As Niles and Deuce cautiously ascended the staircase, the old wooden steps echoed with creaks and cracks, keeping them on edge. Their hearts were pounding, their shirts were collecting sweat, and they both drew their pistols as they stepped onto the 2nd floor landing.

At the end of the upstairs hall, an eerie glow emanated from a slightly open doorway. This was the light they'd seen from the street. They quietly approached the door. Niles pulled it open without ever thinking that it was unusual for a home's interior door to open out into a hallway. Then again, most of Niles's experiences with interior doors had been in schools, where they all opened out.

Niles and Deuce peered into the room. The glow came from a 15-inch tube monitor which flickered annoyingly, the screen of a battered old desktop computer on a work table. On the screen was the generic Windows XP screensaver, the one in which the obnoxious Windows logo bounced endlessly around the perimeter. Niles scanned the room with his flashlight. It was some sort of workroom, with paint cans, rags, gas cans, chemicals, chemistry equipment, and drug paraphernalia scattered about. But there was no sign of Batt-man – nor of anyone else.

They entered. Niles took a closer look at the stuff scattered about the room while Deuce touched the computer's mouse to bring the screen to life. The display showed a newspaper style headline in a big bold typeface:

"HIGH SCHOOL STUDENTS KILLED IN..."

Niles's flashlight illuminated some cans marked "Danger! Highly Flammable!" One of them was leaking – there was liquid on the floor.

Deuce hit "page down."

The next part of the headline said **"...METH HOUSE FIRE CAUSED BY..."**

Niles realized what some of the chemicals were used for.

"Hey, I think the fucker cooks meth here!"

At the same time, Deuce hit "page down" again.

"...ELECTRICAL SHORT." Below were photos of Niles, Deuce and Cam!

Deuce's jaw dropped. "Whoa! Hey, Doug --"

Suddenly electrical sparks shot out from the monitor!

The sparks ignited the liquid on the floor which erupted in enormous flames!

Immediately, the fire caused nearby cans of chemicals to explode. Deuce was sprayed with chemicals and flames! He screamed as his clothes and exposed skin caught fire!

"Let's get outta here!" shouted Niles.

Niles ran out while Deuce tried to extinguish the flames on his body with his hands. Simultaneously, the fire grew as more cans of chemicals ignited and exploded.

Deuce turned toward the doorway, but the door suddenly slammed shut because the air was sucked out of the room by the fire. Deuce tried to open it, but it was no use – it was sealed tight from the difference in pressure. He was trapped!

"Doug! The door's stuck! Help me!!"

But Niles heard nothing. He had already scrambled down the stairs and dashed out of the house onto the street. He turned, expecting to see Deuce behind him, never having realized that he hadn't gotten out. Instead he saw, framed in the upstairs window of the burning room, Deuce – completely enveloped in fire!

Niles stared in horror and gasped as he watched his friend burned alive.

***

In the Workroom, the flames increased until they spanned floor to ceiling. Then, from the fire appeared a hooded silhouette. Not the Grim Reaper, no – it was Batt, wearing a grey hoodie. He was calm, cool, and impervious to the heat. There wasn't even a bead of sweat on him. He made a gesture and the flames diminished.

Batt pulled his hood back and looked around the charred room. He saw the seriously incinerated body face down on the floor. It was pretty gruesome, even by Batt's standards. The Glock was laying beside him.

"Somebody didn't read the sign out front."

He bent down and turned the corpse over to see who it was. "That's three. Now where's numbers four and five...?"

He looked around but found no sign of a number four – then, the sound of a car engine pulled him to the window. He looked and saw Niles's BMW, speeding down the street and out of sight.

Batt was pissed. "Shit!" He kicked some of the paint cans around in frustration. "Why do I keep fucking up?" He sighed. "Jordy, Mitch: sorry, guys, you may not make it through the night."

Chapter 21

Jordy and Mitch had taken a break from playing videogames to do something neither had done in a long time: they put the local news on the TV.

Actually, they had never watched the 11 o'clock news before – it came on after their normal bedtimes. The only times they had watched any local news broadcasts were during tornado watches and other severe weather warnings. But knowing that Kellie was dead was all the motivation they needed to see whether the news qualified for television coverage. It did -- the truck driver, his company and their insurance company made sure of that.

Just as J.B. had said, the authorities were calling it a suicide – well, actually "an apparent suicide" – resulting from internet gossip. A police expert pointed out that there were no skid marks on the road leading up to the crash, so they concluded she had intentionally driven into the parked excavator. And now a reporter was discussing another angle on the story.

"In a related development, Action News has learned that the girl's apparent suicide may have been connected to that alleged teenage prostitution ring thought to be tied to Restaurateur Tommy Rayburn. According to our source, just before she died, Miss

Davies had sent Rayburn a text message that said, quote, I can't do this anymore, unquote."

Accompanied by the words "Recorded Earlier," the TV showed a middle aged man wearing a pink, open collared shirt and some gold chains being escorted by Police from the "Jugs" Strip Club, and then it switched to a man in an expensive suit talking to some reporters as the TV anchor said "Rayburn's attorney, Frank Niles, had this to say..."

The boys immediately realized who he was. "Frank Niles! Whoa – that's Niles's old man!" said Jordy.

"Man, what a tool!"

On TV, Niles made a statement to the press. "My client is a legitimate businessman and completely innocent of these ludicrous allegations. And that's all we have to say at this time."

"I'll bet Niles's old man was doing Kellie, too" said Jordy.

"That's mega-sick."

The doorbell rang. Bagel sat up from where he'd been laying and turned his head toward the front door.

The boys traded a look and checked the clock. 11:10.

Mitch brightened. "It's gotta be J.B.! That means it's all over! We're free!"

The boys eagerly went to the door and opened it, only to have their hopes dashed. It was Cam.

They glared at him. "What are *you* doing here?" demanded Jordy

“I...I came over to apologize...”

“Yeah, right.”

“...and to ask you guys to forgive me for all the shit I've done to you.”

“Get outta here,” Jordy told him. “We're not falling for any more of your bullshit.”

“It's not bullshit, I swear!”

Jordy snickered and mocked him in a falsetto, whiny voice. “'It's not bullshit, I swear.' *Bullshit!*”

“Yeah,” said Mitch, “Kellie came to me just like you're doing, said she wanted to help save my dog. And I believed her.”

“So whatever you're selling, we're not buying.” Jordy tried to close the door, but Cam pushed his way in, desperate.

“Please, guys, you *gotta* believe me! I'm done with Niles! It's over!”

“Why should we believe you?” challenged Mitch. “Give us one good reason.”

Cam thought for a long moment, trying to come up with one. Finally, with tears in his eyes, he said, “because...because I don't wanna die.”

Jordy nodded knowingly with a sigh. “Amy put you up to this, didn't she? Miss fucking goody goody, 'can't we all just be nice.' Well, you tell me something, man. What did me or Mitch ever do to you? I mean, you're the one recording us, putting us on the internet, making us targets. But *why*? Did we, like, ever hurt you? Or call you names? Did we ever rat you out for cheating or for doing any of the shit we know you did?"

"No."

"But now you want us to say 'we forgive you, it's okay that you helped make our lives a living hell for the past year and a half, we understand?' Well, it's not okay and we don't understand!"

"And we don't want to hear any sad excuses, either," continued Mitch. "You did a lot of bad stuff to a whole lotta people besides us, and you can go to hell for it."

Cam dropped his head in defeat. "Okay, I – you're right. I'm an asshole. I've been one for a long time. I figured I had to be somebody else to survive and the somebody I became is a complete and total asshole. I'm not sure who I am anymore, so I can't expect you guys to figure it out." He sighed. "Anyway, if it means anything to you, beyond all the posing and shit, I really didn't have much fun. But listen -- Niles has a gun. Deuce too. And they're drunk and they're pissed, and they might come here. So be careful."

Cam turned to leave, and gasped. So did Jordy and Mitch. *Niles was standing there!* He stepped into the house. Bagel took one look at Niles and darted back to the den.

"Good work, Cam: two for one." Niles looked at the boys with a hard, cruel expression. "All right, stools: where is he? Where's Batt-man? Spill it if you wanna live."

Jordy gritted his teeth and looked at Mitch. "Dammit!

Fucked again!"

Niles barked at Cam. "Grab Wheezer. Hammerlock him. Give him some pain."

Cam hesitated, unsure what to do.

Niles's eyes flashed. "Cam, do what I tell ya, goddammit!"

Cam took a deep breath. "No, Doug. This stops <u>now</u>."

"Excuse me?" said Niles in utter disbelief. "Did you just say "no" to me, motherfucker?"

"That's right. No. N - O."

"Let me tell you something, man: This isn't just us fucking around anymore. Deuce is *dead!"*

Cam's jaw dropped open.

"That's right," he continued. "Burned to a crisp. Batt-man booby trapped that house. Me, I came *this* close. So it's payback time, and these two little stools are gonna pay. But first we make 'em tell us where Batt-man is."

Cam filled with resolve. "No. I'm not doing anything to these guys anymore. I'm out."

"You fuckin' traitor! You were *never* one of us, you chickenshit bastard! Well, you just get the fuck outta my sight, you fag lover! I'll take care of 'em myself!" Niles pulled the Glock from his waistband.

Jordy's and Mitch's eyes opened wide in terror. They were literally paralyzed with fear, too afraid to move.

"The hell you will," said Cam, stepping between Niles and

the boys.

Niles pointed the Glock at Cam. “Outta my way, Cam!”

But Cam didn't move. He stood there defiantly, finding an inner strength he never knew he had. Somehow, he was no longer afraid of Niles. Maybe it was because he had nothing to lose. Maybe it was because he decided that if he was going down tonight, it wasn't going to be as the pathetic sycophant he'd let himself become for the past two years. Maybe it was because of Amy, and that withering look of disdain she had given him an hour ago, a look that said, basically, *you suck.* Or maybe it was because God didn't keep hours and He was busy at work.

Whatever. It was a standoff for a several long, tense, moments, with no one saying anything. Each of their hearts was pounding so loudly they could barely think.

Mitch started to gasp – an asthma attack.

Niles's face turned bright red and he ripped into Cam. “I said, move, dammit!!!”

Cam acted. He lunged for the gun!

As Cam made contact, Niles fired in reflex – *BLAM!* – and the bullet struck Cam in the upper chest!

It felt like the hardest kick Cam had ever gotten, along with intensely burning pain. Cam was knocked backward and collapsed on the floor, bloody.

The boys were horrified – it was like their heads were in a giant echo chamber, and they could barely make out the distant sound of Jordy's mother, calling from the bedroom. “You boys are making too much noise! Turn down that TV! I’m trying to sleep!”

Niles wrapped his left arm around Mitch's neck and pulled him toward the front door. “Outside! If you scream, I'll blow your fuckin' heads off! Move!”

The boys had no choice. Now that Niles had used the gun, they had no doubt he would use it again. They went with him outside, leaving the front door open behind them.

Niles's BMW was parked in front. “You know how to drive, Shrimpboat?”

“Yeah.”

“Then we're goin' for a ride. You do everything I tell ya or Wheezer gets a bullet, understand?”

“Yeah.”

Niles got in the back seat with Mitch, keeping the gun on him. Jordy got behind the wheel.

“Don't I need the key?”

“No, you don't need the fucking key! I got the fucking key in my pants, so all you gotta do is put your foot on the fucking brake and push the fucking start button! I thought you knew how to fucking drive!”

“I do, but my mom's car needs a key in the ignition.”

“Welcome to the modern world, dipshit.”

Mitch was gasping. “I need my inhaler, Doug, okay? It's in my pocket.”

“Then use it, you fucking turd. Anything to stop you from wheezin' on me.”

Mitch pulled out his inhaler and pumped a shot into his mouth. And then another. He could breathe again. For an instant he considered spraying it in Niles's eyes, but he was too scared he'd miss.

“What the fuck, Shrimpboat, start the car!”

“I gotta adjust the seat! I'm a lot shorter than you!”

It took a few tries, but Jordy finally got the seat where he could both see and reach the pedals. Then he adjusted the mirror.

“Start the fucking car, asshole!”

Jordy depressed the brake pedal, pushed the start button and the car turned over. The headlights came on automatically, but he was far too scared to appreciate any of the fine luxuries and conveniences of the “ultimate driving machine.”

“Where we going?”

“You're taking me to Batt-man. You know where he is, right?”

“I think.”

“Then go.”

Jordy gulped, shifted into D and took off.

Chapter 22

Cam was alive. His chest hurt like hell – well, maybe that was a bad metaphor – it hurt with a searing, burning pain, and he knew he was bleeding. But he could feel his arms and his legs, and he could move them, and he could see, so he concluded he was alive. His mouth was dry and his pants were wet. He must have pissed himself and not realized it. He tried to take a deep breath, but it hurt too much, so he took a few short breaths. He heard some light footsteps. It was Mitch's dog, padding over to check him out.

“Hey, doggy, maybe you can get some help?” Cam's voice was weak. He wasn't sure he had enough lung power to call for help, but he'd thought he'd heard a woman's voice a few moments ago. Jordy's mom? The dog was more interested in sniffing Cam's urine tinged pants.

Suddenly, things got darker as a shadow fell on him. The dog backed away. Cam looked up and his face filled with fear. James Batt was standing over him, staring at him intently, with cold, malevolent eyes, eyes that bore, deep, deep into him.

“No!” Cam gasped, “please don't kill me!”

Batt said nothing. He reached into the deep pocket of his

hoodie.

Cam was certain he was pulling a gun to finish the job.

But Cam was wrong. It wasn't a gun Batt pulled, it was a cellphone. Batt punched 9-1-1. The operator picked up immediately.

"9-1-1, what is the nature of your call?"

"Send an ambulance. 2475 Mason, in Westover. Emergency. Gunshot wound in the left lung. Victim, male, aged 16."

Suddenly, Batt was aware of another presence behind him.

Amy. Amy was the doorway. She had just arrived and she gasped on seeing Cam. "Oh my God! No! You – you --"

"No, not me. Not my style. *Niles*."

"Is Cam – is he –?

"He'll live," Batt told her. "Ambulance is coming. But if Jordy or Mitch don't, it'll be because of you."

"What do you mean? Where are they?"

Cam spoke up from the floor. "Niles," he said, in a hoarse whisper. "They're with Niles."

Batt gave her a withering stare that said *you bitch, this is your fault!*

"You have to find 'em, J.B!"

"Duh," said Batt as he left the house.

Amy sat down next to Cam, took his hand and held it tightly. And then she started sobbing. *What have I done?*

***

Jordy was driving toward the house on Glasser Street, hoping against hope that he'd encounter a police car on the way and could ram into it or something – anything to get his attention. Naturally, there was never a cop around when you needed one. No matter, because as soon as Niles realized where they were headed, he slapped the back of Jordy's head.

"Where the fuck do you think you're going?" screamed Niles.

"J.B.'s house."

"He's not there! And the place is booby trapped!"

"Well, I don't know where else he'd be."

"Wasn't he gonna meet you somewhere? Before midnight?"

"I dunno. Maybe my house. We can go back."

"Fuck no! Cops might be there! C'mon, tell me, you gotta know! Where is he?"

"I don't know, Doug!" screamed Jordy in panic.

"It's true," said Mitch. "We don't know where he is! I swear to God Almighty, we don't know!"

Niles pulled out his iPhone. "Then let's call him. What's his number, Wheezer?"

"I don't know that either!"

"No? Well, maybe if I blow your kneecap off, you'll remember!"

"Please, I don't know it, I swear! I don't even have a phone!"

Mitch gasped again as he desperately tried to fight off another asthma attack.

"Niles, no, he doesn't know it!" said Jordy. "But I -- uh -- I got it written down at home. If we can go back there..."

"Bullshit! I ain't falling for that! If you wrote it down, you can remember it! So pull over and start remembering!"

All Jordy could do was bluff while he tried to figure a way out of this mess. He took his time pulling over, trying to think if there was a public place he could easily get to. "Okay, okay, lemme think, it's, uh... 8-6 something. Uh, 8-6-2...3...3...

Niles entered the numbers one-handed as Jordy said them.

Suddenly the phone vibrated in Niles's hand as it played the opening, fateful notes of a familiar tune. The screen showed the image of a grinning Grim Reaper in a hoodie, holding a scythe, with "call from (666) 666-4377. Accept?" Niles stared at it for a moment as the ring tone cycled. It was that tune kids sang on the playground: "pray for the dead and the dead will pray for you." The Funeral March.

Niles swiped the "accept call" button. "*Who is this?*" he demanded.

The phone was in speaker mode so they could all hear Batt's voice responding calmly. "You know who it is, Dougie. You like my ringtone? Chopin's Funeral March."

"I know what it is, asshole! And it's gonna be your funeral!"

"So I understand you dropped by my house. Sorry I missed

you."

"Listen, motherfucker, you're going down, understand?"

"Really. Well come and get me. I'll be at 2101 Spruce Street, right in front of the police department."

"Fuck you!"

"Buck-buck-buck-buck-buck!"

"Hey, dickhead, I got the stool samples here in my car, and a Glock 9 millimeter pointed at Wheezer's head. Tell him, boys!"

"It's true, J.B!" said Mitch. "He's not kidding! And he already shot Cam!"

Niles shouted, "Got it, fag? So if you want 'em to live, you'll do what I tell ya! Are we clear?"

There was only silence.

Niles repeated, "*Are. We. Clear. Asshole?*"

Finally Batt answered. "Clear."

"Good. Meet us at the cemetery, where we were before."

"How appropriate."

"Your funeral. And this time, you're gonna dig your own grave. Oh, and Batt-man?"

"What?"

"If you're not there in 15 minutes, I'm gonna start shootin', and their blood will be on your hands. Are we clear?"

"Clear."

Niles ended the call. He let himself smile, just a little. Finally, he was in control.

Chapter 23

It took about eight minutes for Jordy to drive to the cemetery. He and Mitch had been taken there before for one of the Syndicate's "invitational events," but they'd never been there at night, and Jordy didn't exactly know the way. Niles told him how to get there, and then how to get to the dirt road around the back – it was the only way into the graveyard after dusk. Fog was rolling in, and the place was taking on the appearance of a classic horror movie, with tombstones piercing the ground mist and casting eerie shadows in the moonlight. "How appropriate" indeed.

The unpaved road was rough, full of ruts, bumps, potholes and an occasional crater. Jordy hit one pretty hard, sending them all bouncing.

"Slow down!" Niles barked. "You wouldn't want me to accidentally pull the trigger, wouldja?"

Jordy immediately slowed down.

"No, Doug, sorry."

"Now you're gonna turn right when we get past that big, pink marble crypt up there and then you'll park just past it." Niles leaned forward to get a better view.

That's when Mitch noticed that the pothole bounce had caused

Niles's car key to fall out of his pants pocket. It was on the seat between them, and Niles was so focused on where they were going that he hadn't noticed. Mitch threw a glance at it, then back at Niles, then back at the key. He could probably get it without Niles knowing. But then what? Mitch wasn't sure what he would – or even could -- do with it, but it was an opportunity too good to ignore: better he should have it than Niles. So he deftly moved his left hand over it, gripped it, then switched it into his right hand and put it into his own pants pocket. Niles never had a clue.

Jordy turned right, past the pink marble crypt and parked per Niles's instructions.

"Leave it running and get outta the car," ordered Niles.

Jordy shifted into park, then opened the door. Niles opened his at the same time. It was chilly outside and neither Jordy nor Mitch had jackets.

"Can't we just wait in the car for him?" asked Jordy. "It's cold."

"What, so we can be a nice big target? No way."

They all exited.

"And leave the doors open," Niles told them, keeping his voice down.

Darn, thought Mitch. *So much for being able to lock him out of the car.*

Niles pushed the boys next to each other and then got behind them. "Start walkin'. I'm gonna find a nice ambush spot. And just in case Batt-man tries to take a shot at me, you're my human shields."

"No worries, Niles. I'm not packing," said a familiar voice, behind and above them.

They turned and saw Batt standing atop a mausoleum. Silhouetted by moonlight, he looked every bit the Avenging Angel.

Niles couldn't believe it. "How the hell'd you get here so fast?"

Batt jumped down, ignoring the question. They were about 25 feet apart.

"So what do you have in mind here, Doug? Fist fight? Broken bottles?"

"No. I shoot you where you stand!"

Niles pointed the Glock at Batt and fired -- BLAM! The pistol's recoil surprised him, sending his right arm up in the air.

But Batt didn't flinch. "Nya, nya, ya missed me," he said tauntingly. "You're a lousy shot, Doug, so why don't you just put the gun down? We'll settle this like men." Batt took a step closer.

Enraged, Niles narrowed his eyes in determination, gripped the gun firmly with both hands, aimed carefully, and blasted three more shots at Batt's chest.

BLAM! BLAM! BLAM!

Yet Batt just stood there, as if nothing had happened!

Niles couldn't believe it. But the boys could.

"Number three was the winner," said Batt, unzipping the front of his hoodie. He poked his finger through the hole that the bullet had made. "See that? Right in the heart. Nice shooting. "

"Fuck!" said Niles. "You're not human!"

Batt smiled and took another step closer. "Never said I was."

Niles grabbed Jordy around the neck and put the gun to his head. "Well, *they* are! Take another step and I kill Shrimpboat!"

Batt took another step. "Okay. I took another step. Go ahead and pull the trigger. Be a murderer."

Jordy and Mitch freaked out, terrified.

"Jesus, no, J.B., he means it!" screamed Jordy.

"No, he doesn't." Batt took another step forward.

"Back off," yelled Niles. "I'm warning you!"

"Yeah, I heard you," said Batt. He took another step forward.

Mitch screamed, "J.B, no! What are you doing? Stop! That's my best friend!"

Batt methodically took another step forward.

"That's it," said Niles. "Shrimpboat dies." He pulled the trigger. CLICK! The pistol dry fired. Niles pulled the hammer back and tried again. CLICK!

Jordy was barely holding it together.

Niles tried again with the same result. It was as if there were no bullets in the gun. "What the fuck, it was a full clip! 15 shots!"

Batt chuckled. "Yeah, well, I can have a strange effect on the laws of physics, me being dead and all. Hey, do you know why they call guns 'heaters?'"

The pistol literally started heating up in Niles's hand! In seconds, it was so hot that Niles had to drop it! "Owwww!" There were burn marks on his hand.

Immediately, Jordy wrestled free of Niles and kneed him in the groin.

Niles gasped, then Jordy kicked him in the balls again, harder. Mitch kicked him too.

Niles dropped to his knees in pain. He looked his right palm and saw it was already blistering from the super-heated gun.

Batt came closer and looked down on him with a superior sneer. "Aw, is the hot shit baby boy in hot pain?"

"Look who's on his knees now!" taunted Mitch. "How do ya like the view, Dougie?"

"You look good on your knees, fuckhead," said Jordy. "A lot better than we did."

Batt stepped closer. "I'm thinking that somebody here is ready to do some begging. Is there somebody here who's ready to do some begging?"

Oh yeah, Niles was definitely ready. "Please, don't kill me, man!" he begged. "I'm sorry! I swear, I'll never fuck with these guys again! I'll never fuck with anybody again! Please man, I'm begging you!"

"I dunno," said Batt. "Not very convincing to me. You guys believe him?"

"I sure don't," said Jordy.

“Me neither,” said Mitch. “Epic fail.”

“Please man, I'm not lying! I'll do anything.”

“Anything?”

“Yeah, anything!”

“Okay, then,” said Batt, “why don't you... eat some dirt for us.”

“Eat...dirt...?”

“Yeah. I know it won't be as flavorful as the sandwich you made me eat, but you just said you'd do *anything*. So? Prove it.”

Niles hesitated, and then Batt gave him *the stare*. Immediately, Niles grabbed a handful of dirt and put it in his mouth. He tried to eat it, but he choked and coughed and spit it out. Jordy and Mitch snickered.

“Aw, gee,” said Batt. “You didn't do it. Guess you were lyin'. And if you're lyin', you're dyin'.”

“No, please man, I swear! Don't kill me! I'll behave! I'll change schools! And I'll even go to church and shit!”

Batt shook his head. “Oh, you'll shit. But not in church.”

Niles looked up at Jordy and Mitch. “You guys gotta stop him! You gotta believe me! I'm sorry! I'm really sorry!”

“Yeah,” said Jordy, “you're really sorry all right. A really sorry motherfucker. Who eats dirt.”

“Game over, douche bag,” said Mitch. “We been looking forward to this for a *long* time.”

“So,” said Batt, “it seems the only variable left is, 'Cause of

Death.' Maybe... Gun Mishap?"

BLAM! The pistol suddenly went off on the ground next to Niles, startling everyone.

Batt shook his head. "Nah, too ordinary." He thought a moment. "How about... 'A Freak Accident?'"

Batt made a hand gesture at an overhanging tree. *CRACK!* A large branch split apart and crashed to the ground inches from Niles's head! Niles gasped, and then began sobbing.

But again, Batt was dissatisfied. "No, that's got no irony. Hmmm..."

Jordy and Mitch exchanged a look. They were enjoying this.

Batt snapped his fingers. "Here's a headline: 'Punk Who Thinks He's Hot Shit Gets Burned To A Crisp!'" He made a hand gesture at Niles, and Niles's jacket burst into flames!

Niles screamed!

Batt immediately made another gesture and the flames extinguished themselves. "No," said Batt, "I already did 'Death By Incineration' tonight. Besides, you'll get plenty of fire where you're going."

Niles was a frightened, whimpering wuss now.

Then Batt's face lit up with another idea. "Ah -- but wait, Doug! I seem to recall you don't like dogs. Interesting coincidence: my dogs don't like you!"

With that, three Rottweilers crept out of the misty darkness. They were Hell Dogs, with fierce red eyes and cruel mouths. They approached slowly. Growling. Stalking. Salivating.

Niles was terrified. What could he do? He looked around – and saw his car with the two doors still open and the engine running. *Yes!* He scrambled to his feet and ran toward it. But as he got close, Batt made another gesture: the doors slammed shut and they all locked! And then the engine died.

"No!" Niles screamed.

"Yes!" said Batt.

He smiled as Niles struggled to open the car.

The dogs moved in, fanning into a semi-circle to prevent his running away.

"Take your time, my puppies. We want him to sweat and suffer."

The dogs slowed down.

Niles frantically searched his pockets for his key.

And Mitch smiled as he reached into his own pocket for it, just to make sure he still had it. Should he tell Niles? Should he show Niles? *Oh, yeah.* "Hey, Dougie! Is *this* what you're looking for?"

Niles looked over and reacted in wide-eyed disbelief on seeing Mitch waving the key. "*You* got it?!? Aw, man, you gotta give it to me! Please, Wheezer, have mercy! Throw me that key!"

"My name's not Wheezer, dirtface. D'ya even know what my name is?"

"I – uh – sure – bitch – er, Rich. I mean, Mitch. Yeah, it's

Mitch."

"Wow. You win the prize! Here ya go – catch!"

Mitch threw the key next to one of the dogs.

"Oops. I sure am a lousy throw!"

The dogs snarled at Niles, baring their teeth, ready for the kill.

Suddenly – Niles remembered. He pulled out his wallet. And from it, he pulled a spare manual key. "Ha! I got a spare, assholes!"

Niles shoved it into the driver's door lock and turned it. *Click!* It unlocked! Niles opened the door just wide enough to scramble in, then slammed it shut just before the dogs got to him.

The three Rottweilers jumped on the car and clawed at it, barking like – well, like mad dogs – but they couldn't get in.

Niles laughed. Actually, it was more like a cackle, and he gave them all the finger.

Batt laughed right back. "Hey, Doug? Guess what? I got a spare, too!"

Niles heard a growl from the back seat. He looked and saw an even bigger Rottweiler staring at him – 120 pounds of attack dog!

His eyes widened in horror! His instinct was to open the door, but the other three dogs were jumping against it. Damned if he did, damned if he didn't!

Batt chuckled. "I sure do love dogs."

And then, the big dog attacked.

Jordy and Mitch watched in amazement. The car started bouncing – then they heard Niles screaming (but muffled – the BMW 5-series was a *very* quiet car) – and then they heard the dog snarling – and then some thumping and some other sounds that they couldn't identify. And then there were splatters. Blood splattered onto the car windows.

The Rottweilers outside barked and growled excitedly.

Batt watched with satisfaction.

Finally, all became quiet. The three Rottweilers calmly backed away from the car and sat a short distance away.

Batt gestured. The driver's door opened by itself and the "spare" Rottweiler leapt out, splattered in blood, with something in its mouth. As the dog came closer, Jordy and Mitch could see what it was: Niles's lower left forearm and hand!

"Oh my God."

The dog trotted proudly over to Batt.

"Okay, drop!"

The dog dropped the limb. Batt scratched its head lovingly.

"Good dog, Carl! What a good doggy you are!"

The boys exchanged a look. "Good dog Carl? Really?" asked Mitch.

Batt shrugged and grinned. "I *had* to name him that. I loved those books when I was little. Wanted a Rottie ever since."

"I loved those books too," said Mitch.

Carl joined the other dogs and sat next to them, all in a row.

They looked like the sweetest Rotties imaginable, "Good Dog Carl" times four.

Batt took Niles's Rolex watch off the wrist. It was 11:50. He examined the engraving on the back of the watch face and read it out loud, in a tone dripping with sarcasm. "'Happy Birthday Doug. Love, Dad.' Aw, how touching."

Batt put it on, then looked at the four dogs. "Good job, gang, good job. Are you hungry? Yeah? Okay, you can eat. You earned it."

Batt signaled the dogs, and they all ran excitedly to the open car and jumped in.

Yikes. This was something Jordy and Mitch decided *not* to watch.

Nevertheless, Jordy turned to Batt and nodded with admiration. "That was epic, J.B. Truly epic."

Mitch sighed relief as he nodded in agreement. "Thank goodness it's over."

"But it's not, guys," said Batt. "It's *not* over. Not yet."

Uh oh. The boys did *not* like the way J.B. said that.

Chapter 24

Mitch and Jordy exchanged a confused look.

"Whaddaya mean, J.B.?" asked Mitch. "How can it not be over?"

"Steve Cameron's still alive, but now I can't take him: he redeemed himself when he took that bullet for you guys. If I were to take someone who didn't deserve it, my penalty would be *very* extreme. But I do have this quota," said Batt as he checked the Rolex, "and time's running out."

"Then who?" asked Mitch. "Somebody from the party?"

"Yeah, I've narrowed it down to two, but you guys'll have to call it."

Immediately their minds started racing. They didn't know everyone who'd been there, but there were certainly two of them who had gone out of their way to harass them in the past: "Vomit" Greene and "Big-E" Edwards. But who deserved it more? Big-E, probably – his bathroom "prank" had sent Mitch to the Emergency Room, although even Mitch would concede that this result was unintended. Could they condemn him for that?

Batt continued. "They're two guys, neither of whom called the cops to report a murder, who both took pleasure in the deaths of their fellow human beings, who looked forward to these deaths, who wanted to witness them, who even wanted to help make 'em happen. Two guys whose inner darkness grew with each death, who even refused to forgive someone who asked them for it in earnest."

Jordy and Mitch gulped as they both realized who Batt had in mind. They looked at each other with guilt.

"Us," said Jordy. "It's gonna be one of us."

Mitch closed his eyes. "Oh, Jesus."

"Am I wrong?"

The boys dropped their heads in shame.

"No," said Jordy. "It's true, everything you said."

"I'm guilty too," agreed Mitch. "Big time."

Batt shook his head. He was definitely troubled. "Sorry, guys, I really didn't want it to go down this way. That's why I kept telling you to back off. My plan woulda worked if you hadn't teamed up with Amy. She tipped off Cam. She's the Judas."

Jordy sighed. "Doesn't matter. We'd still be guilty regardless."

"True," said Batt, "but you'd have had time to make it right."

The boys dropped their heads in resignation.

Batt whistled. The four dogs came out of the car and sat dutifully nearby, watching both their master and the boys intently.

"Well," said Batt, "there's a couple ways we can do this. Flip a coin. Draw straws. Or you can both just run for it, see who the dogs get first. You can take a few minutes to decide, there's still time for that."

Jordy and Mitch looked at one another, looked at the dogs and back at each other. They were scared shitless.

Jordy took a deep breath and took a step forward. "No, J.B., just do me now. But could you please use Doug's gun, so it's quick and sudden?"

Batt nodded. "And he'll get blamed for it. Good idea."

Batt made a little gesture toward the gun and the Glock flew up into his hand. He pointed it at Jordy.

"No, Jordy, you're not going!" Mitch told him. "All those years you stood by me, stood up for me when I had my asthma attacks, when you didn't have to. And you were the only one. Well, now I'm standing up for you." He looked at Batt. "Take *me*, J.B."

Batt aimed the pistol at Mitch. Mitch closed his eyes and grimaced, waiting for the inevitable.

"No, Mitch! I'm to blame for this. I got Amy involved. Anyway, it can't be you -- I mean, you gotta take care of Bagel! You're all he's got!"

"You'll take care of him for me. Besides, you got a sister and a mom and they actually care. If you die, it'll cause more grief. Me? Nobody'll care."

"*I'll* care. Besides, you bein' the Wheezer, it's not your fault! You can't help that you were born with asthma. You goin', it's not right. Do me, J.B."

Batt again aimed at Jordy.

"No, wait!" yelled Mitch. "The truth is, well, I dunno, but... what if I really am, y'know, like, gay? I might be, I dunno. So, like, what would I have to look forward to? My life's gonna be a mess. My Aunt'll hate me, and in the end, I'd be going to hell anyway."

"You don't go to hell for that, Mitch." Then, suddenly uncertain, he looked to J.B. for confirmation. "Do you, J.B.?"

"No," Batt assured him. "It's what you do, not what you are."

"See?" Jordy told Mitch. "It doesn't matter. You can still have a good life. Grow up and be a vet. Take care of dogs. Move to New York, or California. So what if you're gay? Lotsa guys are, it's no big deal. You'll be okay."

"Look, maybe I don't wanna deal with it, okay, all the sex stuff? Maybe it's better that I just go out for a good reason. And saving you, that's a damn good reason."

Batt lowered the Glock in frustration. "All right, you two, *stop!* Just shut the fuck up!"

"What?"

"You little bastards are actually willing to die for each other. So I can't take either one of you. Shit! Shit, shit, shit!" He sighed. "Damn, I wish *I'd* had a friend. Just one. Maybe it woulda turned out different for me. Maybe... Aw, fuck!"

He threw the gun into the deepest part of the cemetery. For

just a few moments, Jordy and Mitch could see J.B.'s inner torture over who he once was and what he had now become.

"So now what?" asked Mitch.

"I dunno, man. I don't fucking know. I guess I just go back and explain what happened, beg the honchos to go easy on me. My own fault. Dammit!"

"We'll pray for you, man," Jordy offered.

Batt chuckled. "After what I've done for the past eight years? I don't think it'll do any good. But thanks anyway."

"Well, it can't hurt, right?" said Mitch. "I mean, that's what friends are for."

"And we *are* your friends," Jordy assured him.

"I appreciate that." Batt whistled to the dogs. "Okay, gang: time to go."

The dogs obediently responded and headed off into the foggy depths of the graveyard. Batt turned back to the boys. "When the cops ask, just say it had something to do with some drug deal you knew nothing about, and a hit man with an attack dog. This oughta make it more believable..."

He gestured and the BMW caught fire.

"And guys? Be good."

With that, he turned and walked deeper into the cemetery. In moments, he had disappeared into the fog.

The boys watched him until they couldn't see him anymore. Then Mitch looked up.

"Hey, God? Please go easy on him. I mean, he saved us and he saved Steve Cameron, so that oughta count. And he saved Bagel too."

Jordy looked up as well. "God? What he said. Times a million trillion. Amen."

As the BMW started to seriously burn, they hurried back the way they came.

***

When they were far enough away from the car fire, they slowed down and approached the gate where they entered.

"We'll never see him again, Jordy. Maybe nobody'll ever see him again. It's not fair."

"It sucks, actually," Jordy said.

"Sometimes, I seriously wonder if God knows what He's doing."

"Me too. Once, I saw this graffiti. It said, 'Earth is God's science fair project. He got a C+.'"

"Heh."

As they exited the cemetery gates, they saw headlights piercing the fog. The car slowed down. It was a VW Beetle – Amy's car. She called to them.

"You guys! Oh, thank God you're alive! I was so scared...!"

Mitch scowled at her. "Yeah, we're alive. Just barely..."

“How'd you find us?” asked Jordy.

“Cam's phone.” She held it up. “I went to your house to make sure you were okay and I found him shot, and J.B. was already there and he called 911. Cam said you were with Niles. Cam's got that Friend Finder app so I used it to track Niles's phone. And Niles? Is he...?”

“Gone” said Jordy.

She sighed. “Well...I won't miss him. Not a bit. Look, I hope you're not mad at me for, y'know, telling, but...”

But Mitch was very mad. “He told you to stay out of it, Amy! Big time! I mean, Niles had a gun at my head! And we almost --” He started coughing.

Jordy grabbed him by the arm, held him straight and helped him breathe. “Hey: she did what she thought was right, Mitch. Maybe she *was* right. Maybe... Maybe it was the best thing for everybody, y'know?”

“For J.B.? You think it was the best thing for *him*?”

“J.B.'s *dead*, Mitch. And we're still alive. Didn't you hear what he said? His last words to us? Don't you get it? ”

Mitch considered this a moment, then sighed and nodded. He looked at Amy. “I'm sorry, Amy. It's been a pretty intense night. And I – we – well, we almost – ”

Mitch couldn't stop himself from sobbing.

“I know. It's okay. C'mon, I'll take you home. And look, I brought a friend.”

Mitch looked in the car. Bagel! She'd brought Bagel! His tail started wagging a million miles a minute. At that moment, nothing could have made Mitch happier. His tears of anguish became tears of joy. He climbed into the car and eagerly embraced his best little friend in the whole wide world.

Jordy and Amy smiled, happy to see Mitch so happy.

Jordy got in and Amy drove them away from the graveyard, and Jordy told her everything that had happened. Everything.

Whoa, she thought. *No wonder Mitch had been so upset.* "So: if number five wasn't one of you, who was it?"

"There wasn't any," said Mitch.

"Come on," she said. "There *has* to be a number five. He was so, I dunno, intense about it."

"It's true," Jordy told her. "He said he was just gonna have to go back and explain it to the brass and beg for mercy."

"J.B.? Begging? That's not his style. He must have had, like, a backup plan. After all, it's not quite midnight yet."

Indeed. The digital clock on her dashboard showed 11:58. Arthur Jamison Battaglia did not have to be "home" for another two minutes.

Chapter 25

The three people in the dimly lit bedroom were all nude. The two girls were only 15, but they were very well developed for their age. The man was old enough to be their father. They were in his big round bed in what could be described as a "love suite" which had clearly been inspired by layouts in *Playboy* magazines. The cocaine and the Molly they were snorting was the best money could buy – his money, of course – and the bottle of champagne they had killed was top quality too, Dom Perignon 2003.

They were all laughing and distracted, which is why no one noticed that a fourth person had entered the room. If he'd had more time, he might have watched, but he didn't have time, so he spoke up.

"My, my. You *do* like 'em young, Mr. Niles."

Frank Niles turned in panic to see a figure in the shadows. The girls reacted with shrieks and pulled sheets over their naked bodies in a ridiculous act of false modesty.

"Who the hell are you?" Frank Niles demanded indignantly.

Although the figure stepped into the light, Frank Niles couldn't make out his face because the hoodie obscured it. Nevertheless, the older man realized who the guy probably was and nodded knowingly.

"Ah, Rayburn's boy. Well, I hope you brought the whole 30 grand. I'm not taking this job out in trade."

"Actually," said Batt, "I brought *this*. Got it from your son."

He pulled Doug's Rolex off his wrist and tossed it to Frank. Frank examined it. His face filled with alarm as he recognized the engraving on the back.

"How'd you get this? Is this some kinda threat? Or is Doug in trouble?"

"Yeah, Mr. Niles, he's in a whole lotta trouble. You might say he's in hell, actually. And I don't think even you'll be able to bail him out of it."

"Listen, you: I don't know who you are, but if Doug's in trouble, I demand you take me to him right now!"

"Right now? Okay, you got it."

Batt calmly pulled out the Glock that Doug had stolen from his father and fired a bullet directly into Frank's head. Blood and brains splattered on the wall behind him.

"You're there, dude."

The girls screamed as Frank Niles slumped over, dead.

Batt tossed the gun on the bed.

"And Daddy makes five."

Batt started to leave, then looked back at the terrified girls. They were hyperventilating – so scared, they couldn't move.

"Hey, Girls?" said Batt. "Just a suggestion: consider a

lifestyle change." He winked. "Be good."

He made a hand gesture and the lights went out. The only light left was the glow of a digital L.E.D. clock as 11:59 became 12:00 midnight.

Epilogue

The boys were much happier when they'd learned Doug's Rolex was found in Frank Niles's bedroom. Even Amy was relieved when the boys explained to her that there was only one way it could have gotten there.

In the end, there were only four people who knew what had really happened that night and, even without discussing it, they knew they could never reveal the true story of Arthur Jamison Battaglia to the police, to their parents, or to anyone else.

The intense events of that night gave them a good excuse for not wanting to talk, and for being confused about exactly what happened when they did. And by claiming ignorance and bewilderment over the events, it allowed the authorities to come up with their own narrative. Once Jordy and Mitch and Amy and Cam had a sense of that narrative, they could fill in and confirm a few details that basically amounted to telling the police what they wanted to hear.

Johnny "Deuce" Pullman, a known drug dealer, had been burned to a crisp in a drug lab fire at an abandoned house on Glasser Street. That was obvious, although whether it was an accident or a murder was not. The investigators decided that calling it an accident made for significantly fewer complications and a lot less paperwork, so that's what they called it.

Frank Niles, a sleazy, drug-using attorney with a criminal clientele, had been assassinated by someone with crime connections, possibly Tommy Rayburn, although Rayburn vehemently denied it. Two teenaged prostitutes, witnesses to the hit, blew the whistle on Rayburn's operation, but had been unable to identify the gunman. It was “some guy in a hoodie.” The murder weapon was Niles's own gun, but the only fingerprints on it were those of Niles and his son. The two girls did not recall if the assassin had worn gloves, but it was possible, meaning it was a professional hit. Because the dead lawyer had a lot of enemies, including disgruntled clients and reprehensible characters who had taken the fall for higher-ups on Frank Niles's advice, there was little chance of fingering the mastermind, and even less chance of making a case. And with all of the budget cuts, investigating the murder of a dirtbag whom everyone said “got what was coming to him” would have been a waste of valuable resources.

Niles's son Douglas had clearly been a target as well, as evidenced by the presence of Doug's Rolex at his father's murder scene. Doug's eviscerated remains had been incinerated in a car fire of unknown origin, but most likely set by some sort of incendiary device that had been destroyed by the flames. It was unclear whether the fire was the true cause of death or if the fire had been set to eradicate evidence. Because of the known relationship between Doug and Deuce Pullman, it was surmised that they were part of a drug manufacturing and distribution ring. The involvement of Jordy and Mitch in all of this had been puzzling, but the police ultimately concluded that Doug had gone after them with his father's gun, thinking they had tipped off either the authorities or the hitman or whomever the hitman had been working for. They hadn't, of that the police had little doubt. When Steve Cameron learned Doug was coming after them, he went to warn them and was wounded when he tried to disarm Doug. Doug had then taken the boys hostage, brought them to the cemetery and attempted to make them talk about something they knew nothing about. Then the hitman had shown up with an attack dog, enabling the boys to escape. The boys could offer no clues as to exactly what occurred between Doug Niles and the hitman, much less a decent description of the hitman – just "some guy in a hoodie" – nor could they explain how he had gotten there. Understandably, they ran away from the cemetery as soon as they had a chance. Then, it seemed likely that the dog savagely attacked Doug in the car. At some point, the hitman had managed to get both Doug's Rolex and Frank Niles's Glock from the youth and then, after incinerating Doug – or his remains -- in the BMW, he used the pistol to murder the father. It was all incredibly nasty. No doubt, the two Nileses had really pissed somebody off.

It didn't completely make sense, but it made enough sense to close the case. No one would miss Frank Niles – even his ex-wife didn't attend the funeral -- and Tommy Rayburn would be going to prison, so it was a win-win for the local authorities. Johnny Pullman's death meant there was one less drug dealer in town. And not one person had had anything nice to say about Douglas Kenneth Niles, and not a single classmate of his attended his funeral or sent condolences to his mother.

***

School was a better place for the entire Junior Class without The Syndicate. Other than the four previously noted exceptions, no one knew exactly what had gone down, although a number of kids suspected that "Batt-man" had something to with it, especially because he was never seen again. There were even jokes that the next Batman movie would be Batman versus The Syndicate. Others simply attributed the violent demise of The Syndicate to karma, while some wondered if God's hand had been in it. Predictably, the media did their stories about the "Teenage Tragedy" in Westover, and there was lots of hand wringing by clueless adults and teachers and "experts" who wanted to find some greater societal explanation and then come up with some sort of mechanism to ensure such things would never happen again. Every kid at Woody had the same reaction: *Yeah, right -- good luck with that.*

***

Even before Cam got out of the hospital, he used his laptop and internet access from his sick bed to basically shut down *Hard Woody 411*. He erased every bit of data associated with it, as well as everything relating to James Batt – not only his data, but the school's as well. He considered doing a special *Hard Woody* edition dumping on Doug, but on second thought, decided it was pointless. Cleaning up his act meant, among other things, trying to be less spiteful. So instead, he posted a personal apology for running with The Syndicate and for having been such a jerk, and he promised to be a better person from now on. Amy wrote about Cam's selflessness in trying to disarm Niles on the official student website, so when Cam came back to school, he was treated as a hero. But Cam was no longer interested in being a big shot – life with Niles had cured him of that, along with the unforgettable three word lesson he'd learned as a result: *actions have consequences*. So he went back to being a tech-geek and was a lot happier for it. And he took actions that had far more positive consequences. He helped improve the student website, tutored kids at the computer lab, and gave Jordy and Mitch some of the electronic gear he no longer used, including a 5-year old laptop to Mitch, which Mitch said was one of the best things anyone had ever given him. Cam often ate with the guys in the cafeteria and mended fences with most of the other former targets of The Syndicate. His parents were delighted that his grades improved and that he was more respectful of them. And, to no one's surprise, he began attending church regularly. Being shot and surviving was one sure way to get religion.

***

Jordy's mother, Cindy, had understandably flipped out when the paramedics came to her house to tend to a boy she'd never met who was bleeding on her floor from a gunshot wound, while being comforted by a girl she didn't know, and all of this while her son was nowhere around. Jordy had left his phone to be recharged so she couldn't call him, but the girl – Amy – was certain she could find him and had hurried off to do just that before she could even get a grip on things. *What kind of world were her kids living in?* By default (and because she was an adult), Cindy Hubbard accompanied the wounded boy to the hospital and stayed with him until his own mother arrived. As more information about the events leading up to that night was revealed, Cindy was shocked at her own ignorance about the environment in which Jordy spent so much of his time, and about the bullying to which he'd been subjected. She felt she had totally failed as a mother – it was if she didn't know her own son. And yet, Jordy hadn't blamed her for anything, and assured her there was nothing she could have done. He was now completely confident that things were going to get better at school. Given how things had turned out and the circumstances that had let up to those things, she saw no reason to punish him, because it was clear he hadn't done anything. So she decided she'd cut back on her work hours so that she could spend a little more time with both of her kids or, at the very least, be able to come home without being so utterly exhausted that she'd rather go to bed and pass out than talk with them.

***

Amy Danforth did not get in trouble for being out past her curfew. No one in her house had even known she'd gone out to meet with Cam at Denny's, much less had gone to Jordy's house and then to the cemetery after that. So when she got home, she asked herself, did anyone even *have* to know? She debated whether to tell her parents, but that debate lasted only about 20 seconds and then she woke them up and told them. She told them there'd been a shooting involving some kids that she knew, with a potential for things to get even worse, and that she'd decided she had a responsibility to do the right thing by warning the likely victims. So, she warned them, and helped saved a wounded boy's life, and then helped two other targeted boys get home, and if her parents wanted to discipline her for that, well, that was fine, and she'd leave it up to them. She didn't just get a pass from her parents, she got props. And nothing made Amy happier than getting praise from her dad. He told her that she showed good judgment and a strong moral character, and that he was extremely proud of her, prouder than ever before. He told her he *respected* her. He said it all quietly and directly, in that heartfelt, sincere and meaningful way he had, and it made her feel all good and warm and tingly inside. It made her feel loved in a way she had never felt before. And she hugged him and she cried, and he cried. She hugged her mom too, but it wasn't the same because, well, there's just that special thing between a girl and her dad...at least there is when it was a dad like *her* dad. Then Amy suggested they all pray and give thanks to God for all that they had – which they did -- and her parents decided it couldn't hurt to have a little more God in their lives.

***

The new atmosphere at school was a boon to Jordy and Mitch. A number of kids became friendlier toward them, thanks to Amy and Cam. More importantly, the bullying and teasing dropped way, way back. And when their response to it was, "who died and made you Doug Niles?", that usually sobered up the perpetrator. The boys used the same response whenever anyone called them "Shrimpboat" and "Wheezer," and after a few weeks, those names were a thing of the past. Other kids who'd been bullied picked up the mantra, and it worked for them too. It was liberating for the boys to go to their lockers after school without worrying they'd find a red "invitation." And it was equally liberating to get up in the morning without stress, trepidation or that stomach ache that felt like their insides were all twisted around, and then to ride the school bus without getting "accidentally" hit in the head.

Mitch successfully guilted his aunt into getting him a cellphone. Naturally, she insisted on the simplest option, a "dumb phone" instead of a smartphone, even though Mitch proved to her that there were smartphones available under the lifeline program too. When she was still reluctant, he stood up to her for the first time in his life. "Don't you get it, Aunt Sally? I was being held hostage. I had a gun to my head and I couldn't call or text for help because you were too cheap to let me have a phone. Don't you even care about me? I mean, maybe this is a sign from God that I should have one, and maybe you should listen, because, like, someday, do you wanna explain to Jesus that I died because you were too cheap to consider my safety?" Well, that did it. Mitch got a decent HTC smartphone, and Cam helped him set it up, and finally Mitch was connected and was no longer among the "technologically deprived."

Mitch also got some help from Amy with his wardrobe and grooming. Amy had decided to take on a "big sister" role with him, even though she was less than three months older than he was. "One way to not be a target is to not look like a target," she told him. She showed him the kinds of colors and shirts he should never wear – these were the ones that Aunt Sally got cheap at yard sales – and explained that he should never, *ever* wear a t-shirt that had writing on it or a picture on it or a product on it, no matter what it said or who it was or what it was. "Mitch, you're never gonna look cool, so when you wear a shirt that *tries* to make you look cool, it does just the opposite." She showed him when he should tuck the shirt in (not very often), and how to adjust his pants so he didn't look like a dork, and a better way to comb his hair. At first, she was amazed at how clueless Mitch was about these things, but after she met Aunt Sally and saw how they lived, it all made sense, and she realized that these little things she was doing for him were actually very big things for him and they might really make a difference. And they *did* make a difference, particularly because they helped him feel better about himself.

***

There was now an unbreakable bond between Mitch and Jordy and Amy and Cam, permanently forged in the fire of the events of that night. It was the same type of bond that forms between men in war when their unit is involved in intense action that tests their mettle and resolve. Mitch and Jordy already had such a bond based on their shared experiences of victimization, but it was nice to have two other people they could talk with. And for

Amy and Cam, well, now they *needed* Jordy and Mitch. They couldn't seriously discuss heaven, hell, divine retribution, or J.B. with anyone else, and there were times when they absolutely needed to, and this was definitely not something to do on Facebook. So the four of them found time to regularly get together and have long talks about stuff that really mattered, which also included praying for the soul of Arthur Jamison Battaglia.

Some of Amy's friends thought she had gotten "weird" after that night, especially because she'd sometimes eat with "those guys" in the lunchroom. It troubled her for awhile, but her dad said it was part of growing up, like outgrowing your clothes. He said there were only two guys from his high school he still liked, and that Shakespeare had written about it (in *Henry IV Part II)*, and there was a passage in the Bible about it too: "When I was a child, I spoke as a child, I understood as a child, I thought as a child: but when I became an adult, I put away childish things." Amy printed that one out and put it up in her room.

***

And there was one more thing that happened. One Saturday, Jordy and Mitch and Bagel were walking home after messing around at the Route 12 Junkyard. They always went through the undeveloped bottom land near the creek because Bagel had more things to sniff, and staying off the streets had always meant it was less likely that any of the school bullies would see them. It was dusk. The cooler night air was moving in, the twilight sounds were just starting to be heard, and the ground fog was coming up – ground fog that reminded them of that night in the cemetery. A crow cawed and flew away, and then a squirrel scampered out of the brush and up a tree, and that's when Bagel started sniffing and looking around the way dogs do when something's up. So the boys stopped and looked around but they didn't see anything, so they blamed it on the twilight and the ground fog and they kept walking. But Bagel kept looking and listening, turning his head one way, and then the other, and then Mitch suddenly got the feeling they were being followed – and not by a human. “There's something out there, Jordy.”

Too much had happened for Jordy to presume Mitch was wrong about this, so they stopped and listened, but they didn't hear anything, so they walked some more. And this time Jordy sensed it too. So they stopped again, and they held still and stayed quiet, and *then they heard it.* It was a low moaning sound, with a little gurgle in it. An animal sound. Bagel cocked his head in that direction, and he sniffed. He didn't exactly seem scared, but he didn't exactly seem *not* scared either. So they waited and watched. Whatever it was seemed to be coming from the brush on their left. And then they saw and heard some rustling. It was definitely an animal. It was too substantial to be a bird or a squirrel or a rabbit, and the racoons and possums never came out until dark.

And then they saw it, coming out of the mist. It was big and black, and coming toward them. *A Rottweiler.* The boys exchanged a look. *Whoa! Was it Carl?* They couldn't tell. They'd only seen Carl and J.B.'s other dogs at night. It didn't have a collar, and its eyes were brown, not red. Was it a stray? Whatever, Bagel didn't seem afraid of it. The Rottie padded slowly toward them and seemed as unsure about them as they were about it. They all stood there for several long moments regarding each other. Then Bagel approached it, and the dogs checked each other out. So far, so good – normal butt-sniffing dog behavior. Their tails wagged. Mitch decided to trust Bagel's instincts, so he squatted down, and offered a hand. "Carl? Are you Carl? Hey there, fella. It's okay, I'm your friend. Come, Carl. Come." The dog looked at Mitch and came over to him.

"Is it really Carl?" wondered Jordy.

"I can't tell. He doesn't seem as big as Carl, but maybe."

"Maybe this means J.B.'s around somewhere."

"That would be awesome."

The Rottie came closer and Mitch petted it. He hadn't even been able to tell if it was male or female. But it didn't matter -- it was a dog, and Mitch loved all dogs. The Rottie liked the way Mitch rubbed the top of its snout, so it came closer and licked his face. Mitch laughed. "Good dog! Oh, you're such a good doggy!"

Jordy looked around and called out. "J.B.? Are you here, J.B.? Is this your dog?"

But there was no answer.

The dog rolled over – it was male – and he let Mitch rub his tummy. Bagel got in on the action too: he wasn't about to let this newcomer usurp all of his master's attention. “Yes, I love both of you,” said Mitch, executing double tummy rubs. “I love you both.”

“Maybe J.B. sent him, y'know, like, to protect us?” Jordy suggested.

“Ya think? Can he do that?”

“Who knows?”

Then the Rottie reacted to something and was back on its feet. A squirrel. In a flash, the Rottweiler dashed after it, back into the brush from where it came. Normal dog behavior.

Mitch and Jordy waited for him to come back. When he didn't, they whistled and called out “here, Carl” a few times, but the dog didn't return. They spent the next five minutes calling him, to no avail.

“Maybe it was just a stray,” Mitch decided. “A junkyard dog or something.”

“How many times have we been to that junkyard and ever seen a dog? Any dog? And how many times have you ever seen a Rottweiler around here?”

“Okay, like, maybe never. I'm just tryin' to make sense out of it.”

“I think maybe it was J.B.'s way of letting us know he's

okay."

"Yeah, okay, that works." Mitch took a deep breath. He exhaled, then took another deep breath. And then another. And then several short breaths.

Jordy watched him with concern. "Asthma attack?"

"No," said Mitch with certainty. "Did the air just change or something?"

"No..."

Mitch's face lit up. "Jordy, I can breathe! I can really *breathe*! Whoa, I swear, something just happened – I can breathe!" He stood there, taking deep breaths, inhaling, holding it, exhaling. And he began to laugh. Long, joyful, boisterous laughs as he reveled in the simple act of deep breathing. "I'm not "the Wheezer" anymore! I can breathe! Oh my God, it's so wonderful – I can breathe!"

Jordy laughed too and hugged his friend. Even Bagel sensed that this was something special and he ran around the boys with tail-wagging joy.

Now, medical experts will tell you that some people grow out of their asthma. They'll also tell you sometimes asthma is stress related, so when the stress goes away, the asthma goes away. And these were both reasonable explanations as to why Mitch's asthma went away that evening, never to come back. But Mitch didn't see it that way, and neither did Jordy, although they would never tell anyone, not even Amy. The boys were certain that Mitch's cure had been a gift -- a gift from a friend.

***

Amy spent a lot of time thinking about J.B. She couldn't *not* think about him. He had rocked her world like no one ever had, and there was so much she wanted to know, so many things she wished she could ask him. Where else had he been, and what else had he done? Was he inherently a force for good or evil? She couldn't deny that Westover was a better place "After Batt" than it was "Before Batt," so was he really an agent of Satan? Was it a coincidence that the logo on his shoes, the circle with the three hooks coming out of it, could be interpreted as "666" with the sixes on top of each other, each rotated 120 degrees? And what about the address of his house? If you wrote "4377" upside down, it spelled "hell." And what other names had he used? Perhaps he'd been "Arthur Jamison." Or "Art James." Or "James Arthur." She'd googled those names and other variations, but they were all so common that there was too much to sift through. Perhaps there had there been other "Cams" in other towns who deleted his digital footprint, in which case she'd never know. Most importantly, she wanted to know where was he now, and where would he turn up next? Because she was absolutely certain he *would* turn up somewhere and somehow.

And retribution would follow...

The End...?

Afterword

Retribution High was first conceived and written as a screenplay. I thoroughly enjoyed turning it into the novel you just read, as it gave me the opportunity to get deeper into the hearts and minds of the characters, and to explore areas that are hard to deal with in a film. Nevertheless, I hope that a movie version is in the future. Please visit our website, www.retributionhigh.com for updates, to weigh in on who you think should be in the cast, and if you'd like to see a sequel.

About the Author

Bob Gale is an Oscar-nominated Screenwriter-Producer-Director, best known as co-creator, co-writer and co-producer of *Back to the Future* and its sequels. Gale was born and raised in suburban St. Louis, Missouri, where he attended public high school; he then moved to Los Angeles to major in Cinema at the University of Southern California. He has written over 30 screenplays. His other film credits include *1941, I Wanna Hold Your Hand, Used Cars,* and *Interstate 60,* the latter which he directed. His darker side is clearly seen in the 1992 movie *Trespass*, which he co-authored, and in his episode of *Tales From The Crypt*, "House of Horror," which he wrote and directed. Gale has also written comic books, most notably issues of *Spider-Man, Batman* and *Daredevil*, thus proving to his father that he did not waste hours and hours reading comics in his youth. He lives in Southern California with his wife and their dog, and he still roots for the St. Louis Cardinals.

Retribution High is his second novel (the first being the long out-of-print novelization of his screenplay *1941*).

www.ingramcontent.com/pod-product-compliance
Lightning Source LLC
Chambersburg PA
CBHW061132200626
46817CB00016B/1050

* 9 7 8 0 9 9 1 0 4 1 5 3 4 *